A Bayou

The Story of Darla Gray

By
Eldon Raheem McCraine

Copyright

ISBN: 979-8-89145-908-3   (Paperback)
ISBN: 979-8-89145-707-2 (Hardback)
Library of Congress Control Number:

Front cover Image and book designed by Big Hood
First printing edition 2023
Ancient Wordsmithz Comics and Books LLC

Table of Contents

Dedication

This book is dedicated to all those individuals going through something in their lives. Men, women, and Children dealing with depression and mental health issues. We do not realize these issues and stressors sometimes stem from family trauma and outside sources. This book is dedicated to the fighters, the believers, and those who are considered the underdogs. Of course, I had to pay homage to my mom and dad; Leo and Alice McCraine, they will forever be missed. God blessed me with the gift of words, and I am going to use them to tell my imagination.

"There is always light. If only we were brave enough to see it. If only were brave enough to be it."

Amanda Gorman

Prologue

The streets of New Orleans would never be the same. Darla's name, whispered with both awe and trepidation, echoed through the city's shadows. Her path was one of blood and revenge, as she left a trail of broken bodies and shattered souls in her wake. The perpetrators of her violation became ensnared in her merciless grip, their own sins returning to haunt them with vengeance.

And so, in the heart of the bayou, a tale of darkness and redemption unfolded. Darla Gray, once a symbol of hope and healing, became a force that defied both life and death. Her journey would test the limits of her humanity, blurring the line between justice and vengeance. As her story intertwined with the spirits of the past, the world would bear witness to the wrath of a voodoo priestess who had been reborn in the crucible of unimaginable suffering.

Chapter 1: In the Bayou

Darla Gray had been a malevolent force of nature for longer than anyone could remember. Born to parents of West African decent, she was always in tune with her roots. Her parents came to Louisiana by way of boat in 1869, with a small trade group bringing in supplies from West Africa. They were ship workers (slaves) and once they hit port in New Orleans, they were granted freedom by the captain of the ship. Her father Kofi and mother Abena changed their last name from Diallo to Gray to feel more westernized. They still managed to keep their West African heritage, practicing Vodun, which is a religion practiced religiously by the Aja, Ewe, and Fon peoples of Benin, Togo, Ghana, and Nigeria. This was their native religion with Abena being a powerful Voodoo priestess. She managed to keep it hidden from all in the parish. They couple made their way to Lafourche Parish and settled with Kofi learning from the locals how to gator hunt, which was an important thing in the parish when it came to making a living. Kofi did not make much, but he learned the craft and became one of the best gator hunters in Lafourche Parish. Abena picked up work as a housekeeper for the local town mayor's office cleaning and cooking when needed. The parish town was small and poor, but gator hunting paid enough to sustain a living. Kofi managed to build a hut, small home for his family and after a year of living out there in Lafourche, Darla was born. Her father gave her a West African name Mawu-Lisa, after the Supreme Creator Deity. She was a lovely baby, brown, big eyed and full of laughter and life. She would be well taken care of despite the conditions she was set to grow up in, and her parents

always made sure she was protected and safe. Abena

taught Mawu-Lisa all of her knowledge of Vodou and

made Mawu-Lisa promise to never ever use or display

what she knows, due to the consequences of what may

come from its use. After years of Abena teaching her

Vodou and helping around the house, Mawu-Lisa was

now around the age of thirteen and was starting to

become really good at practicing Vodou without the help

of her mother. Later in that year, tragedy struck. Her

mother and father were murdered by a small group of

racist men from the Klu klux Klan as they all slept in

their little hut in the bayou. Mawu-Lisa heard the noise

and hid in a small space up under the hut, that her father

made for situations like what was happening at the

moment. The men brutally raped her mother and hung

her father from a cypress tree in front of the hut before

stringing up her mother afterwards. Mawu-Lisa was alone for some time out there in the bayou, hiding in her family home until she met her faith at the hands of a racist gator hunter who tried to raid her fathers shed. Mawu-Lisa armed herself with a small cutting axe and yelled at the guy to leave or she would call her father. The man called her bluff and attacked Mawu-Lisa, knocking the small axe out of her hands, and slinging her to the ground. The man then proceeded to rape Mawu-Lisa, as she tried her best to fight him off. Mawu-Lisa clawed kicked and bite at the man, but nothing stopped him from what he was doing. Mawu-Lisa passed out from the trauma and looked as if she was dead. The guy stopped and panicked, got off of Mawu-Lisa and looked for a way to cover it all up. He spotted a can of kerosene and poured it all over Mawu-Lisa, setting her on fire, and burning her alive before leaving her in the backyard to die. It is said that when someone dies in pain and trauma, their spirit tends to become lost and malevolent, angry, and depressed. Lurking in the shadows, her true name, Mawu-Lisa, was whispered with dread and fear throughout the murky Louisiana bayous. It was said that she had been granted dominion over life and death itself from the West African Vodun deities. Her power and wisdom were legendary, though few had ever seen her. Mawu-Lisa possessed the body of a lonely housewife name Darla Crissy Gray and enchanted her with a ritual that locked her spirit inside of the lady body. "I'm Darla now…!!" She said, taking on her new name and body. Darla had found a way to bring herself back to life without aging, but it came at a price. Violent fits of rage and the thirst for death would plague Darla and was always unexpected and uncontrollable. For years and years, she still felt alone and unseen, but that changed one fateful day in the late 80's, when a fisherman

happened to cross her path. He noticed a woman dressed

in black, her face hidden in the shadows of a wide

brimmed hat. He thought little of it and continued on his

way, but suddenly he felt a chill down his spine, and he

stopped dead in his tracks. He slowly turned around and,

to his astonishment, the woman had vanished. In the

same moment, he heard a low rumbling in the distance

and knew without doubt that the mysterious woman was

nearby. Darla Gray had appeared. He slowly backed

away, paralyzed with fear, until he could no longer see

her. But even after she had gone, her presence lingered in

the air like an ominous warning. Everyone who had

heard of her legend now had confirmation of its truth.

Darla Gray was real, and she was a force to be reckoned

with. The presence of Darla Gray in the Louisiana bayou

stirred up a lot of curiosity. People had heard stories

about her, but few had actually seen her in person. But that all changed when word got out that she had a child— a young boy named Leo. It was all speculation, but it was still rumored around Bayou Lafourche. Leo's father was a gator hunter and shrimper by the name of Billy Roe, also from the same Lafourche bayous as Darla. It was during one of his weekend fishing trips that Billy encountered Darla for the first time. From the moment they met, Billy was smitten with Darla, although she wasn't so enamored with him. "Well, hello there Miss Lady, what brings you out here in these bayous if I may ask?" asked Billy, a tall, light-skinned Creole man. "None of your business Sir... Now be on your way!" she replied sternly. Despite her obvious disinterest, Billy carried on chatting and eventually asked her to dinner. "I'll cook something special if you let me have the pleasure of your company," he said as he stepped off his boat onto the dock. "I don't know you," she countered, "so why should I come to your place?" The next day, Billy and Darla went to his house for dinner. His home was a small wooden cabin tucked away on the edge of the bayou. The inside was covered with antique furniture, old books, and trinkets that he had collected from his travels around the world. Billy cooked a delicious seafood meal of fresh oysters, shrimp, and crab for Darla. As they settled in at the dinner table for their meal, Billy began to tell her about his life: his travels abroad, his fishing business, and how he'd come to be living in the bayou. His stories captivated her as she happily listened while they ate and drank wine. Once the evening ended, Darla thanked Billy for an enjoyable evening and said goodbye. But before she left, there was a spark between them that neither could ignore, a spark that would eventually blossom into much more than just dinner companionship. From that day forward, Billy knew he had found something special in Darla, something any man would cherish forever. Soon Darla and Billy's friendship turned them into lovers. Billy never knew much about Darla's past, she never would go deep into her life, and he really didn't care though because he was in love., When asked by the local town folk about who she was, Billy didn't know much to say. He only really knew that she was from Lafourche and was of West African descent. He always thought that she was mysterious and always seemed to know things no one else did. Even though they spent a lot of time together, Darla always managed to keep her true self hidden from Billy. After two years of being together, Darla found out that she was pregnant. Billy was happy and couldn't wait to become a father. Darla wasn't so happy about her pregnancy and even tried a few spells to get rid of the child. It only made things worse for her because it heightens her powers even more. She killed one of the gators in the marsh one day while washing some clothes that was soiled. She ripped the gator open with her bare hands. This scared Darla and drove her into labor. She had a tiny little baby boy and when she looked down at him, she cried. After cleaning him off, she called for Billy. She yelled and yelled as if she was being attacked. Billy showed up and dropped beside her, placing her head on his lap, and picking up his little boy. "Leo" he uttered as he smiled down at Darla, who was weak and covered with fluid and blood. That marked the day of forever for Darla and Billy. The days went by, and Leo was getting to be a big bubbly baby, always smiling and baby talking, but Darla didn't seem right. She seemed distant from little Leo. Billy started to notice when he went to give Leo to Darla she turned away. This would go on for many days until one day, Darla vanished without a trace, leaving Billy to raise their son alone. Billy was able to provide Leo with all he needed and seeing him through school. Despite the fact that Darla had left and never returned, Leo was surrounded by love in his home. He tried his hardest in school and worked hard on getting good grades. He made many friends over the years as well. By the time Leo had graduated high school, he had been accepted into Dillard University, a well-known university far from their small Louisiana town. Billy was so proud of his son who was now making something of himself. He had no idea what ended up happening to Darla, but he knew leaving was her choice and wasn't mad at her for it anymore. At the same time though Billy often looked at his son with an aching heart, wishing even more that Darla could have seen how much of a success her son became and how proud they both were of him. But that day never came as Leo left for college without ever having heard from or seen his mother again. Leo would often have dreams where he would see a woman dressed in black with her face hidden behind a wide brimmed hat, and he knew it was his mother watching over him from afar. No one ever found out what happened to Darla Gray, but those who knew her best knew that her power and influence still lingered in the bayou country long after she had gone. Even today, if you travel through the dark swamps late at night you may just catch sight of her shadowy figure as she watches over those who call it home with an unseen eye.

(Present day)

Leo nervously entered the campus of Dillard University, the realization of everything his mother had sacrificed hitting him like a ton of bricks. He had been accepted with a full ride scholarship and was on his way to getting a master's degree in biology and urban Studies. At first, he feared that he was not smart enough or talented enough to make it at a prestigious university like this one, but now, as he glanced around at the towering buildings and lush green grounds, he realized that his hard work had paid off. He also could not help but think about how his mother would have felt if she had been here today to see him on such an important day. But even though she was gone, Leo knew that her spirit still lingered in the bayou country like an unseen eye watching over him. Suddenly feeling more confident than ever before, Leo proudly made his way towards his classes feeling proud of both him and his mother. No matter what happened today, he knew that Darla Gray was with him every step of the way. It is now the

Summer and Leo took the off time to help his father out back home. Life in the bayou country was a hard one for Billy Roe and his son Leo. It seemed like every day there were new obstacles to face, whether it be poachers stealing their bait lines or storms that threatened to wash away everything they had worked so hard to build. But despite the hardships, Billy always found time to take Leo out into the marsh and teach him what it meant to survive in such a wild place. They would often talk about Darla while they fished or hunted gators, Billy never forgetting the love of his life and Leo getting to know her through his father's stories. Billy told him of how she had been a fearless woman who did not back down from any challenge no matter how daunting it seemed, and he could see that same spirit living in his son as Leo became older. He even started hearing Darla's voice calling out from the marsh on some nights when he was at his loneliest moments, whispering words of encouragement and reminding him that he was not alone. Despite all the struggles they faced on a daily basis, life down on the bayou was still one filled with adventure and beauty—from watching giant gators stalk through the murky waters at dusk to seeing shooting stars streak across an inky sky lit up with fireflies just before dawn. One evening, Billy heard a noise coming from behind his backyard shed. Billy Roe knew the sound of trouble when he heard it and, as he stepped out into the dusk light one evening, he spotted a figure lurking in the shadows by his shed. He went out the back door of his home and grabbed a rake that was resting on the side of the house. As Billy slowly walked around the side of the shed. It was Casey Mason, a poacher who lived just a few miles down the bayou from Billy and his son. He was accompanied by his two sons, Casey Jr., and Jason, and they had all come to take what did not belong to them. At first, Billy was angered that someone would stoop so low as to rob another man's property. Billy yelled out, "Hey, get your ass from out of my cooler and off of my property, before I beat the shit out of you with this rake!!" But then something else crept into his mind: jealousy. Billy seemed better at gator hunting than himself and took much more than he ever could have hoped for on one trip. But still Billy refused to give in without putting up a fight; despite having no legal proof that it was Casey stealing from him, Billy followed the group as stealthily as possible until they reached their destination—another poacher's camp deep in the marshlands. Here at last, Billy was able to confront Casey face-to-face about his actions but instead of becoming angry or violent, Billy had simply proposed a deal. If Casey stayed away from his small farm and stopped stealing from him then Billy would do him a favor whenever he asked for it. Refusing to take no for an answer, Casey. Reluctantly accepted the offer and both men went their separate ways that night—Billy returning home with a newfound respect for poachers like Casey who worked hard no matter how thankless their job may be. From then on life on the bayou changed for both men; while they never became friends, they did develop an unspoken understanding of each other's struggles which allowed them both to live peacefully in their respective corners of the marshland. Things are not always what it seems like in the bayou. The legend of Darla, the Voodoo Lady in Black, was well known throughout the bayou. It was said that she would appear at night and bring death to those who brought harm or trouble to the area. People were always wary when they ventured out after dark, never sure if Darla was real or just a figment of their imagination. Little did they know that Darla was a real person – a woman who had been dead for many years but still lingered on in between worlds, neither alive nor dead. Trapped in her own personal purgatory, Darla had become increasingly depressed and violent as time passed by. Many of the residents believed that it was her ghostly form that caused mysterious disappearances and violent murders that occurred around the bayou. Of course, there were skeptics among the locals who thought these stories were nothing more than superstition and folklore made up by fearful people. But whether or not Darla truly existed did not matter—the fear she engendered kept people away from where they should not be after dark and gave them something to talk about over campfires late into the night. No one knew for certain what happened to poor Darla in the end, but her legend lived on forever among those who remembered her tale and warned others to stay out of places they were not supposed to go—lest they risk becoming yet another victim of the Voodoo Lady in Black. The day after all the excitement between Billy and Casey, things began to get strange for the roe family. Darla was not so happy about what Casey, and his sons did to Billy and was very angry. Around the early part of the afternoon as Casey Jr. was going about his work around the farm, he started seeing a strange figure in the brush just beyond the fence. It was a tall, dark figure shrouded in a long black cloak and it was watching him from afar. He squinted his eyes trying to make out who or what it was but all he could see was an ethereal mist floating in and out of focus. Terrified, Casey ran back to his father shouting "the Voodoo lady! The Voodoo Lady!" Casey Sr. had heard too many stories of the legendary figure known as "Darla" and had no intention of getting involved with whatever she might be up to. He urged his son to stay away from her and never venture into the brush alone at night, warning him that if he did, he may never come back alive. Not wanting to take any chances, Casey Jr. agreed and stayed close by the house for days afterwards, constantly looking over his shoulder for any sign of Darla- or whatever she might be- out there in the darkness of the bayou. Meanwhile Billy had gotten word of Darla's presence in town and decided it was time to find out more about her himself. He ventured deep into the bayou until he saw a small hut surrounded by thick fog and filled with strange symbols drawn on its walls; this had to be where Darla lived! As he crept closer, Billy suddenly heard a voice calling out from inside; it was Darla herself! She greeted him warmly and invited him in for some tea while they talked about her story- how she had been cursed centuries ago by an old witch doctor which trapped her soul between worlds forevermore, neither living nor dead. After hearing her story Billy understood why people feared her presence so much; even though she had never hurt anyone intentionally people were still afraid of her immense power – power that could bring death if used recklessly or in anger. Billy and Leo slowly formed a strong bond with Darla, the Voodoo Lady in Black. But it was obvious to them both that something was not right; Darla had dark secrets that she refused to share with either of them. It was clear that despite her kind nature, she still had an uncontrollable rage within her- one which she could only keep suppressed for so long before it would consume her again. One day, after visiting her hut, Billy and Leo noticed that Darla had disappeared without a trace. Worried for their friend's safety, they searched the Bayou but were unable to find any leads as to where she might have gone. After days of searching, they eventually found her near the edge of the marsh: however, instead of helping them search for food or supplies as usual, she was in a trance-like state –("Salim- A'kiha- Mosona Acoo") chanting strange words in a language neither knew and she surrounded by dead animals hung from trees by their horns. Realizing what was going on, Billy quickly grabbed his son and ran away from the scene as fast as he could. When they got home, he explained the situation to Leo – telling him about how sometimes when Darla gets overwhelmed by an uncontrollable rage she ventures out into the bayous and kills without mercy. He also made it clear that this was why he didn't want them staying there with her too often; he couldn't take any chances with Leo's safety when Darla lost control like this. Still concerned for their friend's wellbeing the two decided to visit Darla more often – hoping that they might be able to help her learn how to sustain control of herself when these urges overwhelmed her again. From then on whenever Billy and Leo visited, they would bring supplies such as herbal medicines or animal skins in order to help her better cope with whatever darkness lurked within her soul. Years passed, Leo is now 28 years old, graduated from Dillard University with a master's in biology and a minor in Urban Studies. At this time, Billy is starting to get a little frail in age. Working around the house and yearly gator hunter has gotten hard for Billy. Leo Started a new job teaching Biology at Southern University of New Orleans and would come down on the weekends from his home in New Orleans to help out with maintenance and food. They two would also visit Darla if time permitted it. On a fateful night at the house, Billy was sitting in his recliner watching old westerns on the T.V. when someone broke into his home through the back door. Billy quickly grabbed his shotgun and walked towards the back door. He saw a figure in the darkness and immediately pointed the gun at them, ready to fire if needed. The figure stepped out from the shadows and revealed themselves to be a young man with tattered clothes, carrying a small sack of belongings. The stranger announced himself as "Louis" from Baton Rouge. Leo had been out in the marsh hunting for gators when he heard the sound of gunshots coming from his father's house. Without a moment's hesitation, he sprinted back towards the house as fast as his legs could carry him – praying with each step that it was not too late to save his dad. When he arrived at the door he was greeted by a horrific sight: Billy lying on the floor, blood pooling around him and Louis nowhere to be found. Leo quickly rushed over to his father and took him in his arms – tears streaming down his face as he realized what had happened. He grabbed a cloth from nearby and tried to staunch the bleeding; however, it was too late – within moments, Billy passed away in Leo's arms. Devastated, Leo rose from the floor and ran out into the bayou – determined to find the person and make them pay for what they had done. He searched for hours with no luck until eventually he stumbled upon Darla's hut in the middle of the marsh. Weeping uncontrollably, Leo told her everything that had happened and begged her help take revenge on the stranger. Darla was silent for a few moments before finally speaking up: "I felt something happening to your father and seen a vision of a stranger. I never seen this man before," she said softly. With fire suddenly burning in her eyes Darla told Leo and motioned for Leo to follow her into the night. Darla instructed Leo to stay with his father until the local police arrived. Darla held her hands up in the air and began to chant an incantation.

("La'Mata- Fa'menta.)

As she spoke, a bright red light shone around her and the waters behind her started to rise and swirl violently. The plants around her started to wilt and die as a thick fog descended upon the area. Soon, Darla was surrounded by Two large hellhounds with glowing yellow eyes. She motioned for the two hounds. They came up to Darla, bowed to her feet and the two of them sped off into the night, determined to find Louis. As they ran through the swamps, Darla instructed the two hounds to stay on Louis' trail. Hours of searching and tracking -the hell hounds are able to sense vibrations in the earth and detect even faintest traces of Louis' passage. Finally, after hours of scarching, they came upon a small shantytown where Louis had been staying. With one swift motion,

Darla dismounted from her hellhound and marched towards Louis' hut – only to find him cowering inside. She demanded that he return what he had taken from Billy's house. Terrified and knowing there was no escape, Louis quickly handed over what he had stolen – a pocket watch that belonged to Billy's late father. Darla took the watch and placed it in the hell hound's mouth. Louis, thinking he was safe, asked to leave town. Darla smirked and said to Louis, "Yes you can," and had one of the hell hound's steps aside so he could leave. As soon as Louis made it to the middle of the yard, Darla said softly. "Sic'em boy!!! The hell hound reacted instantly and proceeded to pounce on Louis as he violently clawed and ate at Louis's flesh until he was ripped to pieces. With justice served, Darla had the hell hound place the pocket watch in her hands before they parted ways – never speaking of what happened that night ever again. Leo was standing by the grave, tears streaming down his face. He had been holding it together for two weeks but now that the day of his father's funeral had come, all of the emotions he had been suppressing came spilling out. Leo's thoughts were interrupted as a bright red light shone through the foggy graveyard. Everyone had gone, while Leo stayed behind. In the distance, Darla descended from a hilltop with two hellhounds in tow. She walked up to Leo and said softly, "Your father would have wanted me here." Leo nodded and embraced her tightly. As they both looked into each other's eyes, they could see each other's pain but also a shared understanding of their situation. With one final look at his father's grave, Leo took Darla's hand and led her away from the graveyard and back home. The next morning as the sun rose, Darla took Leo aside and gave him his father's pocket watch that she had recovered from Louis two weeks ago. Leo took it and held it close to his heart as he thanked Darla for taking care of him and his father, even if it meant putting her own life in danger. Darla smiled knowing that she made a difference in not only Leo's life but Billy's as well – justice being served for both of them in the end. Leo returned to his father's home, he slowly walked up to the front door of his father's house, dreading what he might find inside. He had not been back since that fateful night, and the thought of seeing all the destruction that Louis caused was more than he could bear. Taking a deep breath, he opened the door and stepped inside. To his relief, Leo saw that much of the damage had been taken care of. The broken glass from the window had been swept away and furniture had been put back in place. However, one thing still lingered – Billy's shotgun lying on the floor halfway up under the kitchen table where it slid when Louis shot him. Leo carefully picked it up off the ground and held it tightly in his hands as tears silently streamed down his face. He had come so close to losing everything that day – his father, home, friends – but thanks to Darla, justice was served, and things were almost back to normal again. Leo placed Billy's shotgun beside him as he spent two days cleaning up what remained of the mess Louis made. Although Leo did not want to accept it at first, with time he came to understand that this is how things were meant to be – messy and chaotic but also filled with beauty and love in unexpected places. On the third day when everything was finally clean again, Leo placed a picture frame on top of his father's mantle. It was a photo of himself and Billy fishing on their last trip together before Louis' attack. Leo smiled as he looked at it before placing his father's pocket watch next to it – a reminder of how much they both meant to him and a symbol for justice being served. The next morning, as Leo opened his eyes for another day, he felt strangely content; like something good was going to happen. Maybe it was his father watching over him or maybe Darla's courage gave him hope for a better future; either way Leo knew at this moment in time.

*****

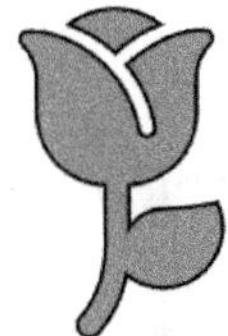

Chapter 2: Something Supernatural

The news of what had happened to Billy quickly spread through the parish like wildfire. Some claimed it was suicide, others said he was murdered and a few even suspected that the Voodoo Lady Darla had somehow gotten him and made him take his own life. No matter what the truth was, everyone in the town was talking about it. Meanwhile, news stations all over were reporting on a gruesome murder that occurred in the parish. They shared details about how the body of Louis was found saying that it looked like a large bear or dog killed him and how some young teenagers, out drinking and smoking weed, stumbled upon the body, and called for help. Fortunately for Leo, this story diverted people's attention away from Billy's death for a while and gave him some much-needed peace of mind. At the scene, Law Enforcement was everywhere, crime scene investigators and the k-9 units were out searching for clues. Louis body was mangled really bad, and blood was everywhere. Louis was unrecognizable and being a drifter, no one knew his name, so they called him John Doe. Suddenly, a black SUV showed up on the scene. Two guys in nice suits with badges and guns got out and made their way to the crime scene. There were agents from the FBI New Orleans division. Agent Debbie Morrison, with the Bureau for ten years and agent Marcus Duncan, in the Bureau for sixteen years and lead agent on the case. The detectives from the Federal Bureau of Investigation quickly took over the investigation, leaving local law enforcement in their dust. With their state-of-the-art equipment and experience with similar cases, they were able to piece together the events leading up to Louis' murder more easily than the local police. One of the detectives walked over to the Lafourche Parish Sheriff officer, Jacob Cannon, and asked to speak to whoever was in charge. Officer Jacob got on his radio and called for Sheriff Conner Ratcliff to inform him that the FBI was on the scene and needed to speak with him. Sheriff Ratcliff was out close to the marsh surveying for clues to what may have happened to their John Doe Louis. The Sheriff walked up to the Agents and introduced himself, " How are you doing gentlemen, welcome to good ole Lafourche Parish, how may I be of some assistance? This is a small-town murder, guys. I can't see this being on the FBI radar." We understand but the crimes of this parish have been on our radar for a few years now. The circumstances behind these crimes are very strange and make no sense at all. We are here to do a follow-up investigation of our own, so we will not get in your way at all. The Sheriff agreed and said to the guys, "our scene is your scene!" as he slides to the side and allows the F.B.I. on into the crime tape. They examined the scene thoroughly for clues and evidence; they noticed tracks which led into a nearby swamp, as well as signs of a struggle such as broken branches and torn clothing. After searching the area extensively, they eventually concluded that the perpetrator was some kind of large animal or monster - likely a wild dog or bear. With no other leads to follow, the detectives focused on finding out who was responsible for this grisly act; did someone hire a wild animal to kill the John Doe? Was it an act of revenge? A gang initiation ritual? Or maybe something else entirely? Agent, Debbie Morrison, stood in the center of the mangled remains of the crime scene trying to make sense of it all. She has been investigating these strange cases for six years now and believes there is something supernatural at play in the parish. After a few minutes of contemplation, she realized that this was not an isolated incident but rather part of a much bigger issue within Lafourche Parish. She also noticed a pattern in recent events - people were being targeted and brutally murdered by a potential predator living in the woods near the small town. With this information at hand, Agent Morrison began her search for clues that would lead to the killer. Meanwhile, Agent Duncan and the local law enforcement personnel scoured through Louis' shack for any evidence that might point them in the right direction.

They found numerous odd objects inside his home, including strange potions and vials with mysterious symbols etched into them. Darla had cursed the shack and any other occupants that move in will meet the same faith as Louis did, death by hell hound. After some intensive research, they uncovered that it was indeed dark magic rituals. Agent Morrison quickly realized this could be the connection they were looking for; however, she needed more evidence before she could draw any solid conclusions. She decided to return to the Louis body to investigate further. After combing through the area, she eventually discovered what appeared to be an animal paw print alongside of some trees near where Louis' body was found - it was here that Agent Morrison finally found her clue; traces of black fur clinging to one of branches suggested there was indeed something monstrous living in these woods. Agent Duncan asked

Agent Morrison if she gathered all the evidence she needed, and she responded, "yes and more!!!" Back at headquarters, Agent Morrison shared her findings and her thoughts on the crime scene, with her team, and they all agreed that there must be a creature lurking within these woods that is responsible for these gruesome murders. Agent Morrison had other thoughts, as she sat at her desk across from Agent Duncan, saying to herself, "Something like that does not happen out of know where, somebody has to be in charge, an owner or handler maybe a Witch. This just does not make any sense!!" After sleeping on it all, agent Morrison decided to return to Bayou Lafourche to do some poking around. She was hoping to maybe get some questions asked about strange things in the area. Without calling agent Duncan and getting him to go with her, agent Morrison packed up her laptop and gathered her duty rig and left for the parish early that morning. Agent Morrison arrived in Bayou Lafourche early that morning and quickly got to work. She began by speaking with locals who provided her with more information about Louis, the Voodoo Lady in Black rumors, and any other suspicious activity in the area. From the conversations she had, Agent Morrison soon realized that there was a woman living on the outskirts of the town who was known for creating potions and performing strange rituals. With this new lead in mind, Agent Morrison drove out to the woman's home to touch base with her. Driving up to the small worn-out shack, a small frail elderly lady was sitting in a beat-up rocking chair on the porch. As Agent Morrison exited her vehicle, and locked eyes with the lady she heard, "So what brings you out here agent?" in a shaky little voice. "My name is agent Morris—" and before she could finish, the little lady said, "Agent Debbie Morrison, yes I know!!" Confused by it all, Agent Morrison put her gun closer to her. "There is no need to be afraid Child... My name is Morgana Weary. I been in this bayou for 85 years now, same spot same home." "So, you would know everything about this area? "Morrison said to Morgana as she closed the door to her vehicle and proceeded closer to the porch where Morgana was sitting. There was a large tree stum next to the porch where Morrison slowly sat down to speak with Morgana where she spoke to her at length about her activities and beliefs. After a lengthy discussion, Morgana revealed that she believed there is an ancient entity locals call The Voodoo lady in black, that prowls the woods and citizens of the parish near her home and was probably responsible for Louis' death as well as numerous other murders in the area. Satisfied with knowing her hunches were not crazy, Agent Morrison thanked the woman for her time and returned to headquarters where she shared what she had learned with her team. Everyone agreed that something mysterious was happening in Lafourche Parish, but a supernatural creature being the problem, has the team a little skeptical. They all agreed though, that whatever it is must be found and stopped before anyone else gets hurt or killed - but how? With no leads or evidence, they were at a loss as to where to start their search. Just then, one of Agent Morrison's colleagues suggested they use tracking dogs to try and locate the creature's den. Although it was a longshot, everyone agreed it was worth trying; so, they made plans to head back to Lafourche the next night to set off on a search with their canine friends leading the way. The night had arrived, and the team was set to go out into the bayou areas to search for anything strange and supernatural. After hours of searching, they eventually stumbled upon an old shack deep within the woods - when they opened its door, they found traces of dark fur scattered around inside - proof that something sinister lurked within these woods after all! Excited by their discovery, Agent Morrison and her team quickly set up surveillance around the shack - determined to trap their suspect once and for all! After several days of waiting patiently, finally one night they spotted a figure emerging from a small gathering of bushes and tall trees. It was foggy and dark in the area due to all the water and humidity. The figure was really misty as it moved with the fog. The difference was this mist was black and moved as if it was a human. It was really animated, as it made its way to the small hut. - it was The Voodoo lady in black. The Dogs went into a frenzy as they coward up and snapped their chains and ran away. They were able to see her true form and also see the Hell Hounds that walked with her. Darla heard the dogs and sent out her

Hounds. "Feed!!" She said to her pet's ad they darted toward the team that was a few yards away. Soon they heard barking coming toward them. They dropped the equipment and took cover, grabbing their aside arms. "What the fuck is that?" One agent yelled as he pointed his gun straight ahead toward the barking sounds. "I don't know, this shit not making any sense!!" another agent yelled as he and two other agents panned out and aimed their guns at the sounds around them. Agent Morrison braced herself against a nearby tree and took in deep breaths. "This was not what I was expecting, how is this possible?" One of the hounds tore into one of the agents, while the other hound snatched an agent into a brush. The other two agents took off into the darkness of the bayou. Splitting up, they ran through marshy water and bushes. "Ugh!!" Yelled one agent, as he was snatched down into the water. Blood squirted violently from the ripples in the water as the agent's head slowly floated up from below. The Other agent came to a tall marshy tree and climbed it. Breathing frantically, she swung her head all around, as fear and death set in on her. Trying to control her breathing, the hell hound slowly crept up being her on the opposite side of the tree. The agent felt the breath of the hound as tears slowly dripped out of her eyes, before whispering, "Help me God!!! The hound dragged his claws across her neck, severing her head from her body as it fell to the earth. The rest of her body was still clinging to the tree with enormous amounts of blood oozing down the tree. By this time, Agent Morrison made her way to the SUV. She opened the door, jumped in, and slammed the door. Grabbing the keys from up out of the armrest, she started the vehicle. She glanced to her left and right as she put the vehicle in gear and drove off. The roadway was foggy and hard to see, as she made a sharp turn in the road, she caught eye of the hell hounds illuminated by the fog. She swerved right and kept driving. When she looked into the rearview, she saw Darla, who was pointing at her, eyes dark read, as her hell hound sat next to her, one on each side. Agent Morrison made it to the interstate, Where she radioed into the Lafourche Parish Police dispatch to report that her team was just slaughtered. Dispatch sent out the call for all available officers to respond to that location along with local S.W.A.T. and CSI. She then went on to drive into the St. Charles Parish Police department, which was the next parish over from Lafourche Parish, to rest and make calls to the FBI headquarters to get immediate back up out to the area. Her call was met with headquarters sending out a team when they are available due to a massive crime scene going on in New Orleans with a serial murdered.

Agent Morrison recouped as she hurried back to New Orleans. Still scared and breathing hard, Agent Morrison started crying as she thought about the lives of her team who were murdered by the hounds. This solidified what she was saying all along, there is something supernatural murdering the citizens of Lafourche Parish. Making it to her apartment, Agent Morrison, covered with blood and marsh dirt, slowly walked to her bathroom. Taking off her clothes and duty rig as she turned on the hot water for a shower. She went back into the bedroom and put her gun on the dresser, while pulling out her bedclothes for the night. As she was putting her shoes in her closet, she noticed a small slash on her arm that was bleeding. She grabbed a small napkin from her nightstand, damped it with water and wiped it off. Her phone started ringing. It was agent Duncan…

(Answers phone)

Debbie: "Hello"

Marcus: "Debbie it is me Marcus, where have you been? I have been calling for you since you left the officer early yesterday."

Debbie: "I got a lead and acted on it… Marcus, it was a disaster. I lost the team, they all died… Marcus. All of them were killed!!"

Marcus: "Slow down… Killed by who, and where were you all when it happened and why didn't you tell me?"

Debbie: (crying) "We were out on the bayou following up on the information I got from the little elderly lady I interviewed. I took the team out there with some surveillance equipment and we set up to try and catch whatever it was killing the citizens out in the bayou. Everything went to hell really quickly. We saw something... something strange, but it also saw us, and it sent some strange looking dogs that attacked us. We could not see them at first but as I managed to get away, I saw them in the fog."

Marcus: "Dogs?"

Debbie: "Yes and they were huge and looked demonic. Their eyes glowed crimson red and teeth were huge."

Marcus: "You need me to come over?"

Debbie: "Would you please, I'm still a little shacking up"

Marcus: "I'll be there in a few!"

Debbie: "Thank you Marcus! Bye"

Marcus: "Ok Bye."

(Hangs up the phone)

Placing her phone on the nightstand, Debbie removes her underwear and walks into the bathroom to shower. The bathroom was really steamy due to the hot water running. Debbie stopped in front of the mirror and wiped away some of the steam to gaze at herself. Feeling overwhelmed and responsible for getting her team killed she wanted to reassure herself and just breathe. As she wiped away the steam, she saw Darla standing behind her with blood coming from her eyes, nose, and mouth as she reached out and grabbed Debbie by the back of her neck and yanked her back towards her before disappearing. Debbie felt jolted back to reality as it seemed to be all in her head. She shook it off and slowly walked into her shower. Lathering up and washing herself, she did not feel the extra muddy hands also rubbing across her body. Long dingy red fingernails can be seen caressing her skin as she continues to wash herself. Through the suds on her shoulders Darla's

hand slid out as Debbie washed and she caught eye of Darla's hand and swiftly jumped out of the shower. Debbie landed on the floor, screaming, and back paddling out toward the bedroom. There was a dark shadowy figure still in the shower that slowly started moving into Debbie's view. "I know who the fuck you are, you bastard... You killed my fucking team and you have been killing citizens out in Lafourche for years. Darla stopped and just stared at Debbie before saying,

"Stay out of the bayou or die... Stay out or die!!!" The lights flickered and went dark, they came back on, and Darla was gone. Debbie, now terrified, quickly got up off the floor and grabbed her gun.

(Knock, knock, knock)

Debbie shuffled over to the door and peered through the peephole. At first, she did not recognize anyone until a familiar face slid into view--it was Marcus. She rushed to open up the door and pulled him inside. Debbie cried intensely as she clung onto Marcus for support. In between her sobs, she told him about the Voodoo lady dressed in black, Darla, who had visited her while she was showering. The woman had warned Debbie not to return to Lafourche Parish or else she would die!! After hearing about her encounter with the Voodoo lady, Marcus suggested they both go back to Bayou Lafourche and investigate further. He said that if the creature did exist, then perhaps they could trap it and end its reign of terror once and for all. Although Debbie was fearful for their safety, she agreed that it was worth trying – anything to protect the people of Lafourche Parish. So, with determination in their hearts, Marcus and Debbie began preparing for their journey back to Lafourche Parish. Marcus requested that Debbie get some sleep, because of all the trauma she encountered and told her they will have to return with Crime Scene to process and clean up the area. Marcus insisted that Debbie get some rest, considering all the horror she had been through. She assented and pulled back the sheets on her bed. Marcus took a few minutes to check the place over, then returned to join her. Sitting beside her, he draped an arm around her in a comforting gesture and told her he would stay close while they were there. Gazing into each other's eyes, they moved closer until their lips met in a tender kiss. They made love and lingered in each other's embrace until morning crept in. Early the next morning Marcus and Debbie laid next to each other under the sheets. "Thank you for staying with me tonight, Marcus." Debbie said as she snuggled close to Marcus. "I wouldn't have it any other way. "Marcus said as he wrapped his arms around Debbie. "We have to get to the crime scene together to go out to that shack where the massacre's happened. Are you sure you can go back?" Marcus asked Debbie as he rose from the bed to get dressed. It was not long before they were packing their bags and driving off with the Crime Scene units in tow. As they drove down the winding roads leading to Bayou Lafourche, they shared stories from their past adventures together – a reminder that even in times of danger, they would always have each other's backs no matter what lay ahead.

(Unit radio chirp: Crime Scene Agent Timothy)

Agent Timothy: "Agent Morrison come in"

Debbie: "Yes agent. What is it?"

Agent Timothy: "We just received a call from headquarters back in New Orleans, that there was another murder last night out in the bayou. A sixteen-year-old girl!!"

(Debbie and Marcus gasped)

Marcus: "Agent timothy, This Agent Duncan, who relayed that call to you?"

Agent Timothy: "Captain Bergeron did Sir... He said it is a mess out there!!"

Marcus: "Damn it... What the fuck is going on in that damn parish?"

Debbie looks at Marcus and says "Something supernatural, I told you that last night... Now do you believe me?" Marcus responds with a confused look,

"Yes I do, and this shit will be a shit show if the news gets ahold of it all."

Debbie: "Agent Timothy, Call headquarters and have them send out more CSI units to the location and let them know we will rendezvous with them after we finish the other scene."

Agent Timothy: "Yes Ma'am Agent Morrison"

(Over... radio silenced)

They all drove out to the shack located in the woods, which was now surrounded with crime scene tape from the local police. As they approached, they could smell a strange and unpleasant odor emanating from the area. "It looks like this is it, it was dark and foggy but yeah this is definitely the place" Debbie said as she stared at the dark shack. The CSI team began their investigation and Agent Debbie Morrison and Agent Marcus Duncan with flashlights in hand, cautiously stepped inside and began to take notes of the evidence they found. The duo carefully perused through every inch of the premises but came up empty handed as there were no other clues that might lead them to their suspect. After a few hours, Marcus suggested that go over what information they had gathered so far. As they stood in the room, Debbie could not help but feel like something or someone was watching her closely from within those walls. Darla took on the form of a dark mist and began to hover over the duo, watching them from the rafters. "I am telling you Marcus; this is the home of that Voodoo lady in black all the rumors are about. This is definitely a supernatural killer we are dealing with right now." As they talked, Debbie could not help but feel like something or someone was watching her from within those walls. She felt a chill run down her spine and told Marcus she thought it might be some kind of dark magic. Marcus, who was more than familiar with such things, suggested that they investigate further. Debbie and Marcus went over their notes from the crime scene while still standing in the room and discussed what possibilities lay ahead in their investigation. Suddenly, out of nowhere, a dark mist began to form in the room hovering above them. "Marcus, do you see that?" Debbie asked in surprise as she stared up at Darla in her ghostly form. Marcus drew his weapon and pointed it saying, "Yes, What the fuck is that?" Darla floated closer to them, her eyes blazing with malice. "You think you can stop me? I am more powerful than either of you can imagine." She cackled, her voice echoing around the room. "You'll never capture me alive!" Debbie stepped forward and said to Darla firmly. "We are here to bring justice for those who have suffered at your hands. We will not rest until we see you destroyed." She brandished her own weapon, determined to stand her ground no matter what happened. Suddenly there was a loud crash as glass shattered and several dark figures appeared from the shadows. It was obvious that all of them were under Darla's control as they advanced on Marcus and Debbie who had their weapons drawn and stances ready for battle. "You don't stand a chance against us!" Darla warned as she launched a large sharp piece of wood at Debbie. Marcus quickly stepped in front of Debbie taking the blow himself, then threw himself on top of Debbie protecting her from any more harm. Debbie and Marcus stood their ground, ready to fight off the dark figures that had suddenly appeared. But before they could even raise their weapons, Marcus moved with lightning speed and shot each figure dead. The entire altercation was over in just a few brief moments. Darla was shocked at how quickly her minions had been defeated and began to back away slowly. "You think you can stop me? I am more powerful than either of you can imagine," she said menacingly as she retreated into the shadows. Marcus turned to Debbie and said, "Well, that takes care of the problem here for now. We need to focus on finding out who this dark entity is and how to stop it. "Debbie nodded in agreement saying, "It is the Voodoo Lady in black. The dark rumors from the residents here in Bayou Lafourche." "Voodoo lady?" Marcus asked Debbie as he dusted himself off and holstered his weapon. Debbie explained to Marcus what the elderly lady from out in the bayou said about the dark spirit that roams the Parish and is the thing that is committing all these murders. Marcus, feeling a little motivated said, "Then it's time we hunt her ass down and end her for good!!" By this time, the CSI agents burst through the doors that were locked by Darla and released when she disappeared. "Agent Morrison and Agent Duncan are you guys, ok? What the fuck was going on in here? We heard the shooting and tried to get in, but the doors were sealed shut and the windows were blacked out and sealed shut too.!!" Agent Martin said as he and Agent Timothy brought in the rest of the team to search the shack. Debbie noticed a small raggedy shed outback that was covered with vines and weeds. They both set off into the shed in search of clues that could help them identify their suspect. They scoured the small area, gathering evidence such as old Voodoo dolls, pieces of fabric with strange symbols embroidered on them, mysterious books written in an ancient language and even a sketch of what looked like Darla's face drawn on a piece of parchment paper. This was an old sketch that Leo did of his mom as a gift to show her how beautiful she was to him. Finally, after hours of searching they stumbled across a diary tucked away in a secret compartment in one of the walls. Inside were pages filled with details about Darla's past along with her real name: Darla Gray. It also mentioned how she was taught by her mother and had studied Voodoo rituals for many years in order to gain more power and control over others. Armed with this added information, Debbie and Marcus knew that they were close to capturing their suspect once and for all. The CSI team Finished up at the crime scene, while the loved one of the agents that were killed were notified of their deaths. The whole team was shaking up over the crime scene on top of the chaos that happened inside the little shack with Debbie and Marcus. After wrapping up the crime scene, it was time to move on to the next one and Marcus had a feeling this one was going to be worse. The local police of Lafourche were near the first crime monitoring the roads and traffic. As the team moved out on to the parish roadway, Marcus stopped the SUV near one of the officers and asked, "Hey Officer Davy, where is the nearest church?" Officer Davy pointed him to the old Holy Savior Church on Main Street near the Bayou." "Thanks sir, you guys be careful out here." Debbie asked Marcus why he needed to stop at a church. He told Debbie, "I got a plan for backup, and he smiled as they took off to the church. The second crime scene involved a young teenage girl named Lisa Wiggins who was out with friends but stayed behind with another young teenager Denim Gracie, who she was in love with. The Lisa has been hiding the fact that she was gay from her family for some time due to her family being catholic. The rest of the teenagers left, and the two young ladies stayed behind to enjoy some alone time with each other. While sitting on a metal beam next to each other, Darla was there hovering over the two as they talked and laughed with each other. They started sharing their true feelings and soon after started kissing each other. Darla had two of her dark entities with her and sent one out to get one of the teenage girls. While moving the entity knocked over some metal poles and made a noise. They stopped kissing when Lisa said, "Denim, did you hear that?" "No!!" Denim said, as they both started looking all around and stood on their feet. "It sounds like it came from over there!!" Denim said as she was then violently swept away by one of the entities into total darkness. Lisa began to call out for her friend and scream, when the second dark entity slowly hovered down in front of Lisa, letting of a low bone chilling growl. Lisa was violently torn to shreds, with blood and parts scattered all over the dark abandoned warehouse. Denim was never seen again and presumed too also be dead.

(Present time)

Marcus and Debbie arrived at their second crime scene in the late evening. They had been told this was an abandoned warehouse by a Shell Lubricant plant, where the teens would go to a party after hours to drink, smoke, and listen to music. They turned on to the desolate road that led to the warehouse, but as they neared it seemed more sinister than expected. The Crime scene had already been investigated and cleaned. The duo decided to wait a little later to go behind and look for anything supernatural that may be tied to the Darla. As they made their way to the entrance, they could feel a cold chill in the air that seemed to walk with them, as if something malevolent was close by. They kept their guard up and proceeded carefully. Just before entering, Marcus noticed a dark figure in the shadows, watching them from afar. Quickly, he moved forward and drew his gun, ready to fire at any moment. Debbie followed suit and held her gun high as she stepped inside. The warehouse was even darker and eerier inside then it had been outside. They found themselves surrounded by tall shelves of old boxes and crates along with strange symbols painted on the walls that none of them could read or understand. In the center of it all sat what appeared to be an altar of some kind with multiple candles lit around it. It soon became clear that Darla had been here recently; her presence seemed almost palpable in this place - as if she still lingered within its walls. Suddenly, a loud noise echoed from behind one of the stacks of boxes and Darla emerged from the shadows. She glared at Marcus and Debbie menacingly as she spoke "You think you can stop me? I will never be destroyed!" She began to cast a spell binding them both so they could not move or speak. Fortunately for them, Marcus had anticipated her attack plan and he had previously brought holy water with him from the old church they visited, which he quickly threw towards Darla breaking her spell over them both allowing Marcus and Debbie to break free of her power once more! Darla retreated back into darkness while muttering sorrowful words under her breath "This isn't over yet." Standing back-to-back Marcus and Debbie kept their guns drawn, with Marcus holding the flask filled with holy water. "I think she's gone now Marcus." "Yes, we won this time... at least for now!! Let us get the fuck out of Killville and take our asses to back to the New Orleans!! Marcus said as he hurriedly walked back to the SUV. The two left for the city, but while going to the access road that leads to the main highway, they passed a small little kid, who looked around 8 years old, standing on side the road with a short elderly woman. The kid was holding what looked like a voodoo doll that was dressed just like him, and he was waving at the two as they passed on by. The child looked strange, flashing a strange grin on his face, while the elderly woman grew taller and younger as they got further and further off. "Yeah, let's get the fuck out of here Marcus!!" Debbie said as they sped off.

******

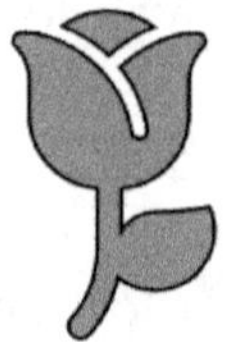

Chapter 3: NOLA Blues

(UNO Campus)

Leo had been teaching at Southern University of New Orleans for several months and relished every moment of it. He had met Alice Williams, a Dillard graduate who majored in History and Theology and was keen on ancient religions and mysticism. They had been seeing each other on and off for two years, and she knew about the mysterious legends from his hometown but had no clue that he was implicated in any of them. Whenever they went out together, Alice would mention stories she had heard about the Voodoo Lady in black from Lafourche Parish. In response, Leo would artfully change the subject or hoodwink her in some way, fearful that she might put the pieces together. Leo loved being able to inspire and shape young minds with the knowledge he had acquired over his lifetime, but all of that changed when he heard the news broadcast about Louis's murder as well as the disappearance of Lisa and her friend Denim. Instantly, Leo thought of Darla and realized there was a good chance she was involved in some way. He knew that if Darla had truly gone off the deep end again then there would be no telling what she was capable of doing. So, Leo decided it would be best if he went back home to Lafourche and talked to her directly to find out what was really going on. Leo took a chance and invited Alice with him on his journey home. He cancelled class for the week and sent out an email to each of his students his students informing them of the change in class scheduling. He then went home and packed up some clothes and a forty. Caliber Glock, he purchased right after the murder for protection. Leo drove home in haste but still managed to keep his cool on the roads along the way back home. Finally, after several hours on the highway Leo arrived in Lafourche. He immediately headed towards Darla's house which looked abandoned from the outside, but he could tell something strange was going on within its walls, nonetheless. Alice asked Leo why they were at the shack and Leo explained to her that his mother lived there. He then went on to explain everything to Alice about his mom and dad's history. The information overwhelmed Alice as she teared up but the History side of her wanted to know more. Leo told Alice that his mom is a part of the spirit world and her

Vodou powers are extraordinarily strong. He also warned her that his mother is probably unhinged and is called the Voodoo lady in Black by the locals. "I knew it!!! I knew that shit was real!!," Alice said with excitement. "Leo looked with sadness at Alice for her excitement. "I'm sorry baby, I just been studying this for so long and you know my passion for our ancestor's history." "So, what are you doing here? Do you think you mother is the one committing these murders?" Leo put his head down and sat low in the seat. "Yeah, I think she's the one doing it all." "Wow!!" Alice said as she caressed the back of Leos's head and gave him a kiss on his cheek. Leo took three deep breaths and got out of the car. He told Alice to stay put and that he was just going to be a few minutes. Alice agreed and he shut the door and made way down the dirt path to the shack. He knocked loudly on the door. Leo was a bit hesitant to enter the house, but he had no other choice but to go in and confront Darla about what was going on. He slowly opened the door and stepped inside, but before he could even take one step forward, Darla had already turned around to face him with an expression of pure terror on her face. "Leo? What are you doing here?" she asked, her voice shaking slightly going from static to anger in tone. "I came here looking for answers. I heard about Lisa and her friend, and I wanted to make sure you had nothing to do with that and that you were okay. I want to help if I can," Leo replied cautiously. Darla sighed and shook her head. "It's too late for that now… things have already been set into motion and there is no turning back." She said sadly before turning away from him again and walking back over to the altar-like table she had been standing at before Leo entered the room. "Leo was stunned as he watched Darla perform her ritual, unable to fully comprehend what was happening. He took a few steps towards her and asked, "What do you mean? Is this why Lisa dead and her friend is missing? What did you do?" Darla stopped mid-ritual and slowly turned around to face Leo; her eyes suddenly filled with fear as she looked at him. She started stuttering and mumbling some incoherent words until finally she exploded into a fit of rage. "Get out Leo... Get out now... I do not want to hurt you Son... Leave now!!" Her voice became gruff, and she began to growl. In the far corners of the room, two dark entities started to ascend from the shadows, their eyes glinting in the faint light of the candles that Darla had lit earlier for her ritual. Leo knew whatever he was dealing with here was far more than he was prepared for and quickly backed away towards the door while trying not to take his eyes off them. His mother had completely lost it and he had to protect Alice who was outside in the car waiting on his return. Leo rushed through the door and ran down the dirt path to the car. Alice had seen him running and was scared as she feared what it was, he may have been running from that was in the shack. "What happened? What did you see?" she asked, her voice quivering with fear and confusion. "Nothing, don't worry, let's just go," Leo said dismissively as he opened the car door for her. He quickly started up the engine and drove off to an unknown destination. As they drove away from Darla's house, Leo explained to Alice what he had seen inside and how his mother seemed to be involved in some kind of dark ritual involving summoning spirits or demons. Alice listened carefully, trying to make sense of it all but ultimately could not make sense of anything other than the fact that whatever his mother was up to isn't something they should be getting involved in any further. With no other answers from his mom on Lisa's disappearance or her friend's death, Leo decided that their best bet would be heading back to New Orleans for now. As they drove along, they both knew that whatever mystery lies ahead will not be easy but it's one they must face if only because the truth is out there somewhere waiting for them to uncover it. On their way back to New Orleans, Leo and Alice continued to talk about the strange events that had occurred. Along the way, they discussed theories and possible answers for Denim's disappearance, as well as her friend, Lisa, death. They also wondered if Darla was deeply involved in some kind of dark ritual. After a long drive, they arrived in New Orleans late at night. They decided it would be best if they stayed at Leo's spot for the time being so they could rest and think more clearly about what to do next. "I'll set up the bed so we can have a good rest, and then you can take a shower," Leo said as he showed Alice where the towels were. "Why don't we just shower together, and then get into bed at the same time?" Alice proposed, turning around to drop her pants and reveal her pink lace panties and toned stomach. Alice was a Goddess, a Concrete flower from New Orleans, her brown skin was earthly beautiful. Leo smiled widely and said in a faint voice "Absolutely!" as he unbuttoned his shirt. His body was beautifully sculpted from working out; being of mixed heritage, his complexion added to his already attractive aura. Alice pressed her body up against Leo as she gently laid a kiss to his lips before they both started caressing each other into the shower. The steam was hot and all over the bathroom as their silhouette showed them slowly making love under the waterfall from the shower. Alice felt her body tingle with pleasure and excitement as Leo kissed and caressed her, running his hands down her back to cup her buttocks and make gentle circles, sending flashes of pleasure radiating throughout her core. Leo took his time exploring every inch of Alice's body, the curves of her hips, the softness of her skin, taking his time in making sure that each moment was more explosive than the last. His breathing became heavier as he worked harder to make Alice feel even more incredible than before. As they continued in their passionate embrace it quickly turned to a euphoric bliss that neither one had ever experienced before. They stayed like this for what felt like an eternity until finally breaking apart, still embracing each other tightly with no intention of letting go anytime soon. They stood there in silence for a while until finally breaking apart with a gentle kiss on the forehead from Leo as he whispered, "I love you" and looked deeply into Alice's eyes - eyes that were now filled with so much emotion it was almost overflowing. Alice smiled, realizing now that this is exactly where she wanted to be - held tightly in Leo's embrace, feeling nothing but love radiating between them both. She knew without a doubt that this was what she wanted to feel forever as she placed a kiss upon Leo's lips before whispering those three magical words "I love you too". The next morning, Leo ran out and purchased some supplies for their investigation into Lisa's disappearance. Leo ran out and purchased the supplies he thought would be helpful in their investigation. He grabbed a few flashlights, a map of the city, and other items they may need such as rope, first aid kit, etc. Alice knew of a local voodoo priestess who may be able to provide them with some knowledge about Voodoo and how to stop it. Alice and Leo made their way towards a quaint shop, situated in the back alleys of town. They knocked on the door and it opened slowly to reveal a tall dark-skinned woman with long hair and an array of trinkets. "Hello 'dere children, my name is Mambo Fatiman, descendant of Cecile Fatiman." "Wasn't she the one who was credited with igniting the Haitian Revolution back in 1791?" Alice said with excitement. "Yes, my child, she is my great, great grandmother. She welcomed them into her store filled with ancient artifacts, dolls, books, potions, and other voodoo paraphernalia. "What Choo you want?" She asked in a broken Haitian tongue.

My boyfriend Leo *(a sudden pause, as Leo stared at Debbie in awe of being called a boyfriend)* has a problem, an extremely dangerous problem. "You mean his mother Darla the Voodoo Lady in Black!!" She is enormously powerful, her roots in Vodou go back centuries. Her blood runs hard through the veins of you my child…" as she puts her hand up under Leo's chin. "You would have been considered a Oungan or male priest. "You can end your mother's terror and free her from the rage that has consumed her if you learn the ways of Vodou," she said with a reassuring smile. She gestured towards two old chairs surrounding a wooden table adorned with small bones on a plate before offering them herbal tea. As she prepared an offering for the gods, she murmured a prayer to ask for guidance on their mission. A stern look crossed her face as she gazed upon Alice and Leo before declaring, "The gods have spoken; you must return to where it all started. Only then will you be able to destroy the evil that has taken hold of your mother's spirit." "Can you teach me Ms. Fatiman? Can you please help me help my mother before she kills again?" "Yes, please ma'am, we need you!!! "Alice second. Mambo took a few steps back and rubber her forehead. "You two are making a big request that I do not think either of us would make it out of. There's just not enough time to get you strong enough or even see if you are capable of learning the ways of Vodou!!"

(Shaking her head and sighing)

"Ok I will help you two, but this will probably get all three of us killed on earth and the afterlife!! We will start as soon as you can get me some of your mothers' old spirituals or writings that were passed down to her. Any kind of incantations or spells she may have written down before she died." Mambo said as she ushered Leo and Alice quickly out of her shop. "Just come back when you have something of hers to work with," and slammed her shop door. Leo and Alice walked away from the store. Their minds are foggy with confusion. Neither of them had expected to find out this much about Darla Gary, but it was a lot for their young minds to process. Alice glanced at Leo as they walked in silence. She could tell he was thinking hard about something, and she knew it must have been difficult for him to hear that dark magic may have overtaken his mother. Alice finally broke the silence. "Do you think it is true what Mambo said? That your mom was involved in…" she trailed off, unable to finish the sentence. Leo nodded solemnly. "I know she is," he answered quietly. I know about someone she killed. A drifter named Louis robbed and murdered my father. My mom set out to avenge his death for her and me. I hid it from everybody because… well because, maybe I wanted it too. He took my father from me, and I wanted him dead too!!" *(Sitting down on the ground crying)* … I have been thinking about this for so long and I feel just as guilty as my mom for it all. I need to stop her!!" Alice sat down next to Leo and placed her arms around him as he leaned on to her shoulder and cried more. Alice bit her lip and tried to think of how she might help him. Then a thought struck her, and her eyes lit up with excitement. "I know!" She exclaimed loudly, making Leo jump slightly "We should go back home and look for something that your mom wrote down or even something that will tell of her roots and aid us in helping free her soul." Leo nodded slowly, mulling over this idea in his mind before finally responding with an affirmative agreement. He knew it was not likely they'd find anything at this point, but he also knew they had no other options if they wanted to try and help him understand more of his mother's power and heritage. Alice and Leo began their journey back to the bayou, with Mambo's words ringing in their ears. They had a mission to complete, and with every step they took it seemed like they were getting closer and closer to the truth of what happened to Darla. For days, they searched through old boxes of mementos in the family home and questioned everyone from neighbors to distant relatives about any information they may have on Darla or her past. But no one seemed to know anything, or at least nothing that was certain enough for them to use. Finally, after all of their searching had been fruitless, Leo decided to take a walk down by the bayou where he used to go fishing and gator hunting with his father. As he walked along the water's edge, he noticed something glinting in the sun—a gold locket wedged between two rocks. This locket had carvings of ritual symbols on the front and back. It resembled the same symbols from the altar his mom had. "This must be my mom's locket, but how did it get out here?" Leo said as he picked it up from in between the rocks. Leo opened the locket carefully and found a small piece of parchment inside. He unfolded it curiously and read the strange script written there: "The power that is mine will be yours one day. You are worthy." Leo did not understand what this meant exactly but he had an inkling that it was something important related to his mother's power and heritage as a voodoo queen. With newfound courage, he tucked the note away in his pocket and headed back to his mom's shack where Alice was still searching. "Alice, look what I found! It must belong to my mom. I remember her also having a diary hidden somewhere!" Leo exclaimed as he held up the glimmering locket that sparkled in the light coming through the worn curtains of the room. "Let us search for it, Leo. Maybe we can still find it!" Alice said as she began examining the broken furniture and closets. Leo paused for a moment, surveying the area, and attempting to recall where Darla had kept her diary. Unbeknownst to them, however, the FBI had already taken the diary when they investigated the home and confronted Darla. The Diary was nowhere to be found, but Leo and his partner did discover bullet casings and a small piece of fabric caught onto one of the rusty nails. "Must have been someone else here. Cannot recognize these holes by the shape of this old place." Leo gathered up another casing, then Alice and Leo decided to go the local law enforcement to see if they had taken anything from their house when they came to investigate. As they walked through the small town, they were met with suspicious glances from the locals who had heard rumors of paranormal activity that had been stirred up by Darla Gary. At the police station, they were met by a gruff man, Officer Danny Murphy who said their department were there to investigate but then the FBI came with their CSI team and took over. We had to secure the roadways while they took care of the scene. It was really weird because they were claiming a shootout, but we still do not know what they were shooting at. Word from them was, it was The Voodoo Lady. A freaking rumor... they had a shootout with a fucking rumor (laughing out loud).

Leo asked who were the agents that were there at the time. Officer Murphy gave them the names, "Agent Marcus Duncan and Agent Debbie Morrison from New Orleans FBI. They were the lead investigators on the case." He then slid Agent Duncan's card across the counter to Leo. He said that they had found some evidence at the crime scene, but they did not know what it was or where it came from. He suggested that Leo and Alice contact the FBI about the evidence that was found. Alice told Officer Murphy thank you as her and Leo turned and left the station. While in the car, Leo told Alice about the folded piece of paper that was inside the locket. Alice asked to see it and Leo handed it to her. "The power that is mine will be yours one day" Alice said as she read the note. Mambo was right, you are the key to stopping all this!! We have to head to the FBI headquarters and speak to both these agents. They both knew that whatever secrets were hidden in this piece of paper could be the key to unlocking Darla's legacy—and maybe even freeing her soul from the evil and rage that is keeping her prison for the last time. It was not long before Alice and Leo arrived at the FBI headquarters. Inside, they were greeted by Agents, hi my name is Marcus Duncan, and this here is my partner, Debbie Morrison. After exchanging names and a brief exchange of pleasantries, Leo explained what they came for: to get access to the diary that was confiscated from his mother's home. The agents looked at each other, surprised by this request but not showing it on their faces. Marcus crossed his arms and spoke first: "Did you say that was your mother's home?" Leo looked and said, "yes, my mother's home. I looked out over her home and my father's home. They were not together anymore but they loved me the same. My Father was murdered and I… My mother is something evil..." Leo said as he hung his head low from shame. Debbie then lowered herself into a nearby chair and gaped at Leo in wonder. "How long have you known about this, Leo? Oh, and by the way, Debbie is fine—I think we are going to be great friends. *(Smirking at Leo)* Getting back to my question: How long have you known that your mother is the infamous Voodoo Lady in Black responsible for all those killings in Lafourche Parish, specifically Bayou Lafourche? Right, her name is Darla. The diary with the initials D.G. found at the crime scene—was that your mom's initials? Did she murder Louis and those teenagers, as well as the other victims? I have known since a child." Leo said as he showed the two agents the locket. "Agents we really need that diary!! Leo maybe the only one who can stop her and what we need may be in the pages of that diary!!" Alice said as she pleaded with both of the agents. "I have to be honest with you two," he said. "We don't often let civilians view evidence in our cases without authorization from the department's top brass." Alice stepped forward, her eyes steely and determined as she stated, "We understand that, but we really believe that the diary may hold something crucial to freeing his mother's soul. We're not asking for much; just a chance to look through it." Marcus nodded slowly before turning to Debbie, who gave a small nod in agreement as well. He then turned back towards Alice and Leo, giving them an affirmative response. "Alright then," he said with a sigh of resignation, "You can come back tomorrow morning at nine when I will have the diary ready for you." The next morning, Alice and Leo returned to FBI headquarters with anticipation in their hearts. When they entered the office, Marcus and Debbie were already waiting for them with the diary on his desk in front of him. Marcus handed them both gloves so as not to leave fingerprints of any kind inside of it before allowing them a careful examination of its contents. As they browsed through its pages, they found spell after spell written down alongside diagrams; all left behind by Darla as evidence of her magical prowess. Leo and Alice took a deep breath and slowly reached for the diary, putting on the gloves Marcus had given them. They carefully opened the first page, where Darla's initials were written in bold letters – D.G., confirming that this was her diary. Alice began to read out loud some of the spells and diagrams she found in it. She was amazed by the power these dark rituals could possess and how much power Darla had over it all. Leo studied more as he went, finding out that each spell had been carefully crafted with different ingredients, chants, and symbols that created powerful magic when combined. They read on further until they came across a page with some names listed: Louis, Mercy, Elliot - all victims of Darla's voodoo magic - followed by a plan for something bigger and more sinister. They looked at each other in horror as they realized what it meant; their suspicions about her past had been correct all along. Marcus interjected by saying that they would need to investigate further to make sure no other victims were there before taking any action against their mother. He assured them that they were safe there and offered to take them to get something to eat from the café downstairs so they could calm down from what they had just discovered. Alice agreed immediately but Leo hesitated; he wanted to stay behind with the Agents and look through the diary for anything else useful that might help them understand what was going on or put an end to his mother's schemes for the last time.

Marcus nodded in understanding before continuing on his way with Alice, leaving Leo and Debbie alone with the diary one last time... Leo and Agent Duncan started poring over the diary to find any clues that might lead them to the truth. They flipped through its pages one by one, studying the intricate drawings and symbols that Darla had used in her spells. Debbie looked, her eyes glistening with tears as she thought about the victims and their families. "Leo...I think your mother is responsible for all these deaths, not just Louis's," she said quietly. Leo nodded, understanding what had to be done. He took out his phone and began making some calls, hoping to find someone who could help them unravel this mystery and bring justice to those affected by his mother's sinister plans. Meanwhile, Debbie flipped through the pages of Darla's spell book and discovered a particularly powerful ritual involving human sacrifice - something she knew would need to be investigated further before deciding how best to proceed. He also found records of Darla's travels throughout Louisiana, New Orleans in particular - something which could prove essential in uncovering more of her story. After a few hours of studying the diary together, Leo and Debbie met back up with Marcus and Alice, who bought some food back from the café for them to eat. Leo briefed Marcus and Alice on what they found, and they ate. Afterwards they call it a night, left the building feeling drained but determined - they knew what they had to do next: put an end to it before anyone else was hurt or killed. On their way back to Leo's place, Alice questioned if he was prepared to present the agents to Mambo and if she would be willing to take them on in stopping Darla. Alice brought up that Mambo was one of New Orleans' oldest Voodoo priestesses and may not care for law enforcement near her business. Leo glanced over at Alice and said yes, though they had to risk it. They finally arrived back at Leo's place, and he quickly gathered the items needed for their meeting with Mambo. He readied himself to go back to her shop where they would meet her and presented his plan. He explained that a Voodoo Priestess like Mambo has the knowledge and insight into Darla's powers and activities that they could never possess alone. He also pointed out that despite her reluctance in dealing with law enforcement, Mambo was a respected figure within the community who always acted with integrity. Alice nervously bit her lip, knowing how risky it was to put all of their trust in someone who effectively operated outside of the law. Nevertheless, she agreed to accompany me. him and support him in whatever he decided was best for them both. Leo phoned Debbie late at night and explained that he had someone knowledgeable in Voodoo who could assist her. He also suggested she may not want police officers around when they arrived the following day. She responded by confirming she would meet up with Marcus to greet them and requested Leo text over the meeting place address and time. Alice looked at Leo before they turned in for the night and asked, "Are you sure you are ready to do this, take on your mom?" Slowly placing his hands on both her cheeks, Leo responded. "Only if you are by my side the whole way!" as he kissed her on her forehead. She smiled and returned the kiss before wrapping her arms around him tightly. They embraced each other for a few moments before heading to bed together. As they laid down on the bed, Alice could feel Leo shaking slightly as he processed all that was ahead of them. Gently stroking his hair, she whispered, "It's going to be okay, we are going to do this together" and leaned in for a passionate kiss.

******

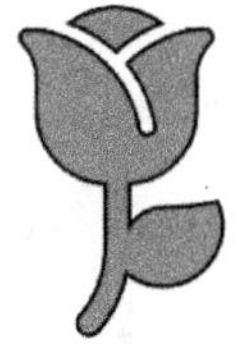

Chapter 4: Siren in the Night

The morning came too quickly and soon they were getting ready for their meeting with Mambo. As they drove there, Alice could feel Leo's nervousness growing with each passing mile but when they arrived at the old house where Mambo lived, he seemed to find some strength from within himself. Leo knocked upon the door, and it opened slowly revealing Mambo wearing traditional Voodoo garb. She thanked them both for coming and welcomed them into her parlor. Marcus was already there waiting along with Debbie, who had accepted the invitation after all. For hours they discussed Darla's activities in New Orleans and how best to move forward in stopping her schemes for the last time. After looking through Darla's diary, Mambo looked very, very scared. She told the crew Darla mastered her craft but gave in to something sinister. "Leo, your mother was relying on an immensely powerful book from an ancient Sangomas called The Handbook of Ritual Power. It is being held by the South African Collector Jabari, who inherited it from his father. This organization is called Apex 8 and has been credited for their invention of nano technology that some say is magical. You would have had to go to Johannesburg, South Africa to even get the book, but it is impossible to enter the grounds of the organization. They have a massive amount of armed personnel guarding the place. Luckily for them, Mambo knew someone knowledgeable enough about it, without the need of the book. She was located out of the country. She then filled a bag with seven of her protection oils and gave them to Alice. Mambo also gave them a name, Masego Mahlangu. "Seek out this Powerful Sangomas. She will definitely be able to guide you. The crew left the shop with everything Mambo gave them and went to their homes for the night. "In two days, we start our journey to ending the madness in Lafourche Parish, Leo said to Alice as they drove off onto the interstate. Marcus asked Debbie was she ready for whats about to happen and she said, "yes and I've been waiting for a long time to see and experience the supernatural!" Marcus smirked saying "Woman you are weird as hell... Pretty and crazy!! As they both laughed while driving off.

(Back in Bayou Lafourche)

Sirens blaring, strobes flashing as Officer Derby Gats is in pursuit of a small hatch back stolen from an elderly lady's front door.

Officer Derby: "Dispatch...

Dispatch 212: "Dispatch 212 go head!!"

Officer Derby: "I am going to need backup for this pursuit. Vehicle is traveling at 75 to 80 miles an hour down Hwy 90...

Now we are going off road ... I need more units to ascend on Hwy 90 and the sheet metal shop on Old Main Street Rd."

Dispatch 212: "Copy that sending two units to your twenty... Dispatch 212: "Dispatch 212 to Unit 428 and 434... Respond to Old Main Street Rd. I repeat... Old Main Street Rd... Chase in progress... Officer in need of backup!!"

Officer Derby followed the suspect down Old Main Street until they reached a dead end. The area led to the swampy areas of Bayou Lafourche, and they had come to the end of the road. The suspect jumped out of the vehicle with Officer Derby in pursuit on foot after calling for back up. He chased after the suspect, who jumped through patches of grass and mud as he tried to lose him. As Officer Derby closed in on the suspect, his boots sunk into the mud and slowed down his movements, while the suspect's own footsteps were quiet enough to free himself. He felt something stick to his boot and looked down and saw thick dirt, which made his movements stealthier now that it stuck around him like a shell. He stopped feeling things when he got one good look at the trees ahead of him. They all spread out wide with their branches in every direction as if making a pathway across a meadow. With each step closer he took; more and more branches would break off and fly through the air toward him as if they were alive. Out of instinct, he turned around and ran away from them as fast as he could, feeling something touch his hair but not being able to see what it was due to everything moving too fast or he could not turn around because there was no space between him and a tree trunk. He noticed that none of these branches flew over or near the wooden shack surrounded by bushes by the water that stood in front of him. He ran into a hut and closed the door behind him just as hundreds upon hundreds of branches flew through the air, blocking out all light inside! He sat breathing heavily, wondering what this place was - why he was here – or where he was? "Who else is here and why did you help me?" There was an eerie quietness as he asked again, "Who are you; Why did you help me? Show yourself!" A door on the far side slowly opened, revealing an old fashioned white lovely looking lady with fair skin who spoke softly saying if he wasn't hurt, she could help him hide out for a while. The suspect felt a chill enter his bones as he studied the dilapidated shack. There was something about the look of the decrepit structure that made him uneasy. "Why is this exquisitely beautiful creole woman living in this cursed place?" he muttered, backing slowly toward the window as she moved closer and closer to him. He could smell his own fear, and soon they were nose to nose. "I can help you free yourself from your troubles!" she purred, her voice dripping with malice. He could feel the evil emanating from her like a fog. Trembling, he asked, "Are you the Voodoo Lady who kills?" Tears streamed down his face as Darla paused for a moment, then whispered coldly "Yes… I am." In a single swift movement, she tore open his throat and clawed at his chest until he lay still in a pool of blood. Officer Derby emerged from the brush seconds later, only to be confronted by the horrific scene inside the shack. He noticed the broken branches scattered on the ground, and his heart sank as he slowly stepped into the room. He was met with an eerie silence, which intensified upon finding a dead body lying in a pool of blood. Staring into Darla's eyes, he realized that she had been the one responsible for the killing. Officer Derby quickly called for backup and ran from the Shack. Darla's wrath descended upon Officer Derby as his feet flew over the ground, desperately trying to escape her.

His lungs burned and sweat stung his eyes with every step he took while the trees raced past him in a dark blur. But it was not enough to shake Darla's pursuit. A sudden hush fell over the marshy area and Officer Derby looked around cautiously, assuming that he had lost his pursuer. However, when he turned around to move forward again, there stood Darla with an icy glare in her eye; her hell hound just inches away, its fangs glinting menacingly in the moonlight. With one word from its master,

(Ser-Vista)

its claws sprung out to attack, lacerating Officer Derby until he was paralyzed in a trance of terror. The Other Officers arrived to find the two cars at the end of the rode. The area was now foggy and very dark. The officer shouted an urgent call to dispatch:

(Radio transmission)

Unit 434: "434 to Dispatch 212. We are in pursuit of a suspect and require assistance!!"

Dispatch 212: "What is your location Unit 434?!"

Unit 434: "428 and I are 10:23! We need back up and medic stat! Suspect is on foot, elusive and dangerous - hurry!!"

Terror filled the air as the officers pinned their hopes on their support arriving in time.

(Transmission clear)

The two officers cautiously followed the faint footprints in the mud leading into the marsh, aware that they were heading deeper into darkness with no clear idea of what they would find. The fog grew thicker, and their visibility decreased as they continued on their search. As they rounded a corner, they came across a frightening sight: Darla's hound standing guard over Officer Derby's lifeless body. Instinctively, both officers reached for their guns and prepared to fire. But before they could act, Darla emerged from the shadows and shouted "STOP!" in a voice that shook the very air around them. Without hesitation, the officers complied, despite not knowing what to expect from her next move. With an unwavering gaze, Darla declared "You will not take me alive!" With that she raised her hands, opened her palms, and began to chant in ancient languages while blue flames radiated from her body. Frightened but determined to protect one another and bring this mad woman to justice, the two officers fired. The bullets bounced off of Darla's ethereal body as she cackled with delight. With a wave of her hand, her two hellhounds were unleashed, tearing after the officers who were retreating to safety. The officers fired their final shots in desperation at the hounds, hoping against hope that they could survive this and escape unscathed. But it was too late. Their hands trembled in fear as the monstrous beasts bounded through the dark, wet wooded area. In a desperate attempt to save themselves, the officers split up and ran in opposite directions. Little did they know that another pair of hounds lay hidden ahead - patiently waiting. In a matter of seconds, one officer had been mauled mercilessly, While the second officer was attacked and clawed to death. Their screams, ringing, went out into the night air as Darla laughed wickedly at their plight. It was three police officers and the carjacker that had been brutally killed by Darla's hand, while the stench of death permeated the marsh air. Things sat still until the backup arrived. Everything started happening fast, as all nine police units, including K-9, plunged into the darkness to find the bodies of their fallen comrades. As they searched desperately for any sign of life, the radio crackled with urgency "Come in dispatch– There's no one in sight and a search must be conducted!!" said one of the officers as the medics followed closely behind, ready to tend to the wounded should they miraculously be found. It was a tense and solemn moment as each of the police units went in search of their fallen comrades. There was an eerie stillness throughout the marsh as all nine units searched silently in the darkness. Every so often, a voice could be heard on the radio reporting back with news of no avail - no sign of Officer Derby, the suspect, or anyone of the other officers. With heavy hearts, they all continued their search. Suddenly, a loud yelp echoed through the night sky followed by frantic barking. The K-9 unit had found something, and everyone rushed to the location to investigate further. The medics were ready in case there was still someone alive who may need their help and when they arrived on scene, they found Officer Derby dead. The scene was an unearthly nightmare;

viscera and entrails were strewn like confetti, smeared in pools of coagulating blood. The dogs' howls filled the air with a cacophonous terror, as they located the other two officers who had been brutally ripped apart, in a scene so horrific it could cause the strongest heart to shudder. The police officers had no choice but to bear witness to this sight, for though it scared them, they knew their duty lay in apprehending whoever did this and bringing them to justice. With the remaining officers gathered around Officer Derby's body, their faces grimly determined, they began the lengthy process of searching for any clues that would lead them to her whereabouts. One of the officers saw a small house hidden by the trees and called for some of the other officers to assist with investigating the place for more clues as to who committed this brutal murder. Other officers on the scene could be heard in the distance, saying that they had heard rumors about the voodoo lady in black with her devil dogs roaming near this section. The officers then approached the old shack slowly, and one of them peered through the broken window, spotting a horrific sight. The walls of the room were smeared with blood and dismembered body parts lay strewn about the floor. With a determined look in his eyes, the same officer kicked open the front door with one swift motion for them to get inside, revealing a grotesque scene: the carjacker was shredded beyond recognition, his flesh half devoured. Shocked silence overtook the officers as they surveyed the carnage before them; one of them stifled a gasp while another ran outside to vomit, covering their nose and mouth with their arm. he officers were appalled at the carnage before them. It was clear that whatever had been responsible for this horror was greater than human strength; it must have been some kind of supernatural force. As the CSI team arrived on the scene, they began combing through the evidence and taking photos of the gruesome scene. Meanwhile, several local news crews had drawn wind of this tragedy and had made their way to the crime scene in order to document what they could. Even though they had no tangible evidence as yet to point towards a specific suspect, the name, Voodoo Lady in Black, kept being whispered among the police officers as they discussed what could have happened here. The CSI team finished up their investigation and concluded that whatever had torn apart these poor souls was far more powerful than human strength; it must have been some kind of supernatural force. A grizzled lead detective, Archie Davis of the Bayou Lafourche Police Department arrived at the scene. His 20 years of experience had hardened him, and now there was a glint of steel in his eyes as he commanded further investigation into the mysterious Voodoo Lady in Black and her devil dogs. After some deliberation, it became evident that this was not just an urban legend – someone was going around using the myth of the Voodoo Lady in Black to commit murders. The killer had to be the trainer of powerful beasts, using them to rip apart their victims in a matter of seconds. So, Archie and his officers split up, searching for any clues left by the killer and their animals. Then one group followed a trail of blood leading from the crime scene to a small clearing in the woods - where they uncovered an abomination beyond their wildest nightmares... There they found several items of interest: an old cauldron with strange symbols inscribed upon it; animal bones scattered about; and a book filled with bizarre recipes dealing with dark magic. As the unit stepped into an unknown clearing, a chill ran through Detective Davis's spine. Before them was a horrifying ritual of voodoo being performed by an old Black woman draped in a robe that seemed to move with its own dark energy. As soon as she noticed the officers, she spun around and uttered a few strange incantations before disappearing into the night.

(Mang-gada Relentah Sigmata Delmetata)

The sight left all the officers in awe and confusion, as they gazed upon the altar of human skulls and body parts that lay before them. "Detective did you see that?" one officer said, trembling in fear and excitement. "No," Davis replied with aggression in his voice. It was obvious he was lying due to his ignorance and beliefs. "I think our killer is here somewhere." The news teams were soon at the scene, bringing with them bright lights and cameras. "I'm Carol Langley, with late-breaking news," she said as her microphone was thrust towards the detectives. "I am now standing at the crime scene, where four people were murdered. The location is Bayou Lafourche. According to reports, three officers from Lafourche Parish were involved in this tragedy as well as another individual discovered inside an abandoned shack in the bayou." As she spoke, some of the locals gathered around them; some shaking their heads in disbelief, while others whispered about dark rumors, they had heard of a mysterious Voodoo Lady in Black. It seemed like almost everyone in town had heard some kind of story about this woman and her pets – but until now no one had taken it seriously. "We've also learned that there aren't any leads," Carol continued, "and some out here are saying this was the work of some drifter or towns person using the myth or rumored of the Voodoo Lady in Black to commit these sick murders." Detective Davis was getting furious because of all the news crews showing up broadcasting. "Will someone clear these fucking pests off of my crime scene..." He growled. "Please!" The officers looked at each other and then back at him, taking a step backward so as not to draw his attention. "I Want them all gone!" he said with his teeth clenched. "Yes Sir!" one officer replied, and they both walked over to two separate news reporters. They quickly escorted them off the property and directed their teams to get back in their vans and drive away. It took hours, but after the officers were able to get rid of all the news crews and once the CSI team finally wrapped up. Now after a long night of police work, the officers from the Bayou Lafourche crime scene drove back to the station in exhaustion and grief. One by one they climbed out of their vehicles and made their way inside. Once they were all settled in, Detective Davis called a meeting to discuss what to do next. "We need to find out who this suspect is as soon as possible" He said with a heavy heart, "We must reach out to the families of our fallen brothers and inform them of what has happened. We also need to get the DNA results from the suspect found in that shack so that we can identify them and hopefully put an end to this mystery." Everyone agreed on his plan and quickly got to work gathering information on the family members and sending off the blood samples to get DNA results from the labs in New Orleans. Detective Davis gave Sheriff Ratcliff a call to inform him that they units had made it back to the station and he was ready to give Sheriff Ratcliff a briefing on the carnage. After several hours of meeting with all of his officers, Sheriff Ratcliff realized he had to get back in touch with Agent Morrison and Agent Duncan. They had managed to piece together a name for someone who may be able to shine some light on the situation. Their Person of interest was Leo... The officers immediately began searching for his last known address or whereabouts but came up empty handed; Thinking he had vanished into thin air. They did not know he didn't use his father's last name Roe, but used his mother, Darla's last name Gray. Just when it looked like all hope was lost, Detective Davis had an idea; he remembered hearing stories about an old, abandoned cemetery on the outskirts of town where some people had seen a mysterious woman in black walking about late at night. He thought to himself; it was worth a shot anyway, so he decided it was time for another visit that old cemetery in the back of Bayou Lafourche with his team in tow, but before he goes out, he was instructed by Sheriff Ratcliff to wait for words from the FBI agent, Marcus Duncan, who was out in Baton Rouge following leads for a Drug Cartel murder of a Government Official, a case and he took on while Agent Debbie Morrison was out of the country with Alice and Leo. The next night, Detective Davis was extremely bothered by the fact that he had to wait to visit that cemetery. So, he decided to just take a drive past it to maybe see if he could get a glimpse of something strange. As he pulled up outside the cemetery, Detective Davis could feel something strange in the air; something eerily familiar yet unfamiliar at the same time... "Something just not right about all of this." As Detective Davis pulled up to the abandoned cemetery, his heart raced with fear. He had heard rumors of a Voodoo Lady in black who had been seen walking around the grounds at night and it was this same lady that some said was behind the mysterious murder and disappearances of adults and children in the area. He clutched his gun tightly as he slowly crept out of the car and leaned against it, looking around cautiously for any signs of life; but all he saw were tombstones—

old and new alike— standing tall amongst the overgrown grass and weeds. Suddenly, something caught Davis's eye; a small figure in a black cloak walking towards him! He ducked down behind his car and watched as this woman came closer, her cloak dragging on the ground behind her. She seemed to be muttering something under her breath. Davis held his breath, not wanting to make any more noise than necessary. As she approached, he could make out what she was saying… "Leo… Leo… Where are you, my child?" His curiosity piqued further, he decided to take a chance and followed silently after her as she walked into an abandoned mausoleum at the far end of the graveyard. Peering into one of its small windows, Davis could see inside— shelves filled with strange symbols and drawings that looked like voodoo symbols… Whatever this woman was involved in was definitely something suspicious. Davis's heart raced as he silently counted the seconds until he knew she was gone. Just then, a loud howl filled the air and Davis felt the hairs on his neck stand up. Gripping his gun tightly, he mustered up all of his courage and stepped through the doorway, ready to confront whatever was inside. As his eyes adjusted to the darkness, Davis slowly turned around only to see nothing. But when he looked quickly to his left, an enormous Darla Hell Hound snarled and growled at Davis with its menacing yellow eyes. Davis froze in place, terror coursing through his veins as the giant hound loomed closer. He could feel its hot breath on his face and knew he had nowhere to run. The Voodoo Lady in black had left him here— to be attacked by this seemingly indestructible creature! Davis trembled uncontrollably, his body shaking as he slowly raised his gun, barrel pointed straight at the beast. The creature seemed to sense his hesitation and growled menacingly in response. With a gasp of fear Davis pulled the trigger and the deafening sound of gunfire erupted within the mausoleum walls. Suddenly the Hell Hound was gone, leaving Davis alone in the darkness with nothing but the voices of the dead rising from beyond the walls. It sounded like an army of ghosts had converged around the mausoleum, ready to take revenge on those that disturbed them. Davis stumbled out of the mausoleum, his entire body shaking with fear. He could still hear the dead whispering all around him, their voices echoing in the night air. It sounded like an army of ghosts had converged around the mausoleum, ready to take revenge on those that disturbed them. Davis turned and ran back towards his car as fast as his legs would carry him, but as he rounded the corner, he came face-to-face with the same Voodoo Lady in black who had lured him into this situation. The woman immediately stepped forward and raised her hands, casting a strange spell that paralyzed Davis in place. She began to chant something in a language he could not understand, and soon enough Davis could feel a powerful force taking control of his body and mind. The Voodoo Lady's voice rose like thunder, with a roar that shook the very ground. Her words were sharp and filled with rage. "You have crossed a line and disturbed the eternal slumber of our ancestors! Now you shall pay for your intrusions!" She thrust out her hands towards Davis, sending forth a raging inferno that engulfed him in an instant. His mouth opened in a sorrowful scream as he felt the searing heat of the flames licking every inch of his body, until suddenly it was gone, leaving only an empty patch of blackened earth while standing right in front of his car. "I got to get the fuck out of here"!! Davis said as he quickly started his vehicle and left the cemetery.

******

Chapter 5: Pancakes and Fangs

The following morning Detective Davis called the Sheriff to give an update. As Ratcliff heard his story, he felt that the situation could be getting worse. After ending the call, Davis went into the bathroom to prepare for the day. He has a wife named Kimberly and two kids: an 8-year-old son, Melvin, and a 12-year-old daughter, Davina. Finally, after cleaning up, he made it over to have breakfast with his family. The family sat that morning enjoying some grits, eggs, and bacon, with toast and pancakes on the side. Kimberly bought out some cold orange juice in a pitcher and sat it on the table. Archie fixed him and Kimberly some coffee and they all sat down to eat. "Archie, don't forget to pick up Davina and Melvin after school today!" Kimberly said as she sipped her coffee. "I won't, I can't forget about my cubs!" Archie said as they all laughed. Archie put a strip of crispy bacon into his mouth and chewed for a moment before speaking. "We are having a guest tonight, so clean your room and make sure you do your homework as soon as I bring you back home from school today." He took a sip of his black coffee. "Ok dad!!" The kids said as they grabbed their book sacks and hurried off to the bus stop to catch the bus for school. Kimberly put her long blonde hair up in a ponytail and turned to face Archie as he placed the last of the supper dishes in the dishwasher. She had been thinking about what to prepare for dinner, knowing Archie would want one of her specialties. "Whose coming over tonight honey?" she asked. He could tell by her tone that she already knew the answer to this question. "I invited Sheriff Ratcliff over to talk about a case from work." Archie responded as he scrubbed his hands with the sponge. "Oh great" she said with sarcasm. "Guess I better whip up some meatloaf, since that's all he talks about!" It was clear to Archie what she was hinting at; he ignored it. "Honey," he said softly with a smile on his face, "you know he loves your meatloaf." While they were in their home, outside in a thicket of bushes lurked the hell hound. It had grayish black fur and lanky legs. Thick muscles rippled beneath its skin as it moved through the bushes. It was clear that Darla sent the hound out after Archie and ordered it to kill him. Archie flew through the front door, panic in his eyes. He barked orders to Kimberly to retreat upstairs, and hastily dragged furniture and other objects from around the house to barricade the door shut behind them. His hands trembled as he pulled two pistols from their holsters, thrusting one into Kimberly's hands while locking his gaze upon hers. "You know how to use this sweetheart?" he asked urgently. "Y-yes!" she replied quivering with fear. She asked desperately what they were running from, but there was no reply as Archie reached for his phone and dialed 911.

(Phone ringing)

Sheriff Ratcliff: "Hello Detective Davis," his gruff voice echoed down the line, "it's kinda early, is everything alright?"

Archie: "Hell no!" he screamed, a mix of desperation and anger tainting his voice. "I need some units here quick! There is a huge beast trying to kill us!!"

Sheriff Ratcliff: "A beast? Are you sure? What does it look like?"

Archie: "Fuck what it looks like sir, just send help!!!" His voice cracked as he hung up the phone and dropped it onto the ground.

Sheriff Ratcliff knew something was terribly wrong, so he ordered an immediate response from dispatch. He grabbed his gear and raced out to Detective Davis's home himself.

Sheriff Ratcliff flew through the streets. He was not sure what he would find when he arrived at the Davis residence, but he knew it was something serious. His heart thudded in his chest as he screeched to a halt outside the house. The sheriff jumped out of his car and raced to the front door, banging loudly on it. "Detective Davis! Are you there? Open up!" His voice was full of urgency as he pounded on the door again. Suddenly he heard a loud crash followed by gunshots coming from inside the house. He pushed against the door with all his might until it finally opened just enough for him to squeeze through. He found Detective Davis huddled behind a couch with Kimberly crouched next to him, both armed with pistols and terrified expressions on their faces. The room was in chaos; furniture and shattered glass scattered across the floor like confetti. Sheriff Ratcliff quickly assessed the situation and immediately realized what had happened--Archie was right. Something big, some kind of animal had broken into Archie's home and was now trying to break in again! He grabbed his own gun from his holster and ordered Archie and Kimberly to stay put while he investigated outside for any sign of the beast. As soon as Sheriff Ratcliff stepped out onto the porch, he saw a large grey shape lumbering away from the house towards a nearby thicket of trees. He fired several shots at it but missed each time, knowing that if he hit it, it could kill him or someone else if it retaliated. Sheriff Ratcliff returned inside, his heart pounding in his chest. He had not been able to find the beast and feared it had escaped. He quickly checked on Archie and Kimberly, who were huddled together on the couch. They both appeared shaken, but unharmed. "Are you two, okay?" Sheriff Ratcliff said, his voice gruff with emotion as he put a hand on each of their shoulders. "I'm sorry I couldn't get to it in time." Archie nodded and embraced Kimberly tightly. "We'll be okay," he said softly. "We just need to figure out what to do next." Sheriff Ratcliff agreed, as Davis suggested that Kimberly go stay with her mother in Algiers with the kids until they figured something out. Kimberly nodded reluctantly and went upstairs to pack her bags while the sheriff contacted dispatch to have a unit come by and pick her up. Once she was gone, Sheriff Ratcliff and Archie sat down to discuss their options. They decided that until the beast was caught, they would station an armed officer outside the house for protection at all times in case it attempted another attack. Then they began planning a trap for whatever creature was lurking in the shadows of Detective Davis's home. All of a sudden, Sheriff Ratcliff said, "We really need to get them FBI agents involved as seeing they know more about whats going on!" Yes, because I'm not losing my family and my life over this!!" Archie said as he sat bake in his chair.

"We will set up some CCTV coverage around your home until then, I will call Agent Duncan from the Bureau. Sheriff Ratcliff made the call and contacted Agent Duncan, but he wasn't in the office. I will continue to reach out to him Archie!!" The sheriff said as he ordered two of the camera techs to recheck all of the security cameras. After several days of surveillance, one of the cameras captured footage of a large, grey shape walking through a meadow near Archie's home. The agents rushed to the scene, but by the time they got there, whatever had been there had vanished without a trace. Realizing that their prey was clever enough to evade them once again, they decided it was time to act decisively - something needed to be done before anyone else got hurt or killed by this creature.

******

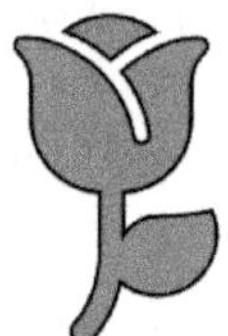

Chapter 6: Deep Roots

The crew were on their way to Johannesburg. Their flight landed and Debbie was able to get a guide to take them to the village of Shangana. Alice asked the guide if there was an information center to get maps of the region just in case they wanted to explore more. The guide suggested they stop at the Airports Tourist Information Center to get all their needs. "Could you give us a few minutes to look around before we leave out?" Leo asked the guide. "Yeah., I don't mind, as a matter of fact, take your time!!" As he sat down in a lobby chair and read a local magazine. The group left and made their way to the Information Center, when Debbie noticed a mysterious-looking shop across the street. From the outside, it was obvious that this was a store of ritual items, potions, spells, herbs, and spices. "Hey everyone, let's go check out that shop!" Debbie exclaimed with enthusiasm. Leo and Alice were both interested and followed her back to the guide. After informing him of their plans to visit the shop, he retrieved his things before parking his vehicle in front of it. He told them all, "I'll stay here until you are finished." The group made their way to the entrance of the shop. Debbie looked up at the sign and initials carved into it and could make out "V.P." – she knew these must be the initials of Voodoo Priestess in this area. She opened the door and was met with a sweet smell that immediately calmed him down. The room was filled with shelves full of glass jars containing various liquids, powders, stones, plants, and more. An incense burner hung from the ceiling which continuously spread its enchanting aroma throughout the space. Leo and Alice were amazed as they scanned items with curiosity; they had never seen so many magical supplies before! There was a bookshelf and an old table with books and picture folders along with old pictures in frames that were unhung. Alice started looking through the books that were of spells and different rituals, while Leo and Debbie were looking through the old picture books and picture frames. "Hey ladies check this out?" Leo pulled up an old photo of two women, dressed in ritual clothing, in front of a small fire pit and an old hut Leo said to them. "Look closely. I mean real, real close!! The lady on the right resembles my mother. Alice and Debbie peered closer at the photograph, astonished to see the resemblance between Leo and the woman in the image. "Oh, my goodness!" Debbie exclaimed, "This is incredible and frightening at the same time!" Alice put her arm around Leo and whispered, "You sure do have an interesting history!" As they turned the corner, a kindly older woman greeted them with a smile that crinkled her eyes and offered them herbal tea. The aroma of mint and chamomile drifted into their noses and warmed their insides. Alice asked if she knew about The Handbook of Ritual Power. The shopkeeper's gaze became unfocused, as if she were transported back in time to a place she would rather forget. Her face twisted into an expression of horror and betrayal. Her lips trembled before she spoke, "That book is cursed! It brings nothing but pain and suffering to those who seek it." She paused to catch her breath before continuing, "You should leave this place at once and never return!" The air around them suddenly felt thick with tension, like a storm cloud on the horizon. Debbie quickly jumped in saying, "Ma'am we are so sorry about that, we are just looking to gain some... "Stop child... I can spot a lie before you speak it!!" She introduced herself as Asma'u, owner of this Voodoo shop. "I'm from a long line of Priestesses and Sangomas," she said. "I overheard you talking about your mother after looking at that picture. "If that is your mother, I think her mother comes from Amarachi Diallo's family." Leo responded by looking at the photo again and confirming this. "Yes, my grandmother's last name was Diallo before it was changed when they migrated here. They named my mom Mawu-Lisa before she switched it to Darla." Asma'u explained that Mawu-Lisa is a Supreme Creator Deity in Vodun belief and was immensely powerful, thus hinting at her daughter being highly influential too. When asked where Darla currently was, Leo informed her that she had become flooded with destructive rage and evil intent and now caused harm to innocents, accompanied by terrifying hounds. "Hell Hounds!" Asma'u said in fear.

With urgency she advised them to seek out a Sangomas who could help ease Darla's spirit and take away her intense negativity. They asked the shopkeeper about a Sangomas named Masego Mahlangu. "Yes, I know her… She is a very powerful Sangomas and knows the Handbook very well. She gave them directions to Masego Mahlangu, before wishing them luck on their quest. Alice and Debbie thanked Asma'u for her help before they departed from the old Shop. As they followed the directions which she had provided, Alice's mind was clouded with doubt. It seemed like every step further away from home was taking them closer to a future that had yet to be defined or revealed to her. Still, they trudged on, determined to find help for Leo's mother. After a long journey, they came across the small village called Shangana, tucked away in the forest. The air smelled of fresh brick and bread, of smoke and spice and the sweat of honest labor. Children ran through the streets playing tag and singing songs about their lives together while parents tended to their gardens or chatted over glasses of sweet tea behind open windows. After asking around, they soon found themselves at the doorstep of Sangomas Masego Mahlangu. Her home was a small hut with trinkets made of wood and glistening stones hanging on the outside. A small wooden chair was perched on one side of a large wooden bucket, which looked like where she washed her clothes and food. A small fire was still twinkling with embers that spat out smoke every now and then; it had burnt down to the last bits of log. Leo gently tapped on the door. (Knock knock) The door then creaked as a small voice of a child said "Who are you? What do you want here? "Leo answered softly, "Ah, we are looking for someone named Masego Mahlangu. We need her help." An oppressive silence hung heavily in the air until a stoic figure appeared at the door. Sangomas Masego Mahlangu, the local Vodun Priestess, looked at the three with an intensity that could split boulders. Her eyes were as deep and wise as they were shrouded with sadness. When Alice softly spoke of being sent by Asma'u to help them, Masego seemed to hesitate before she opened the door wider for them. Masego welcomed them inside and gestured for them to sit around the small fire. She poured them cups of hot herbal tea and sat with them, listening intently to their story. They told her about how Darla was consumed by negative energy, transforming into something dark; how fear-inducing hounds accompanied her; and how they believed Vodun was their only hope to undo it all. When they finished, Masego's eyes were filled with an emotion that seemed to be a mix of sadness and understanding. She looked at each of them with the same intensity as before she spoke. The air tasted sweet and brimmed with quiet strength. "It is not easy," she began in a voice that was both gentle and strong, "to confront the darkness we have created within ourselves or within others. But if you are brave enough to do so then there is always hope." Masego then explained that she had been expecting their arrival since she felt a rift in the spirit realm a lot of years ago. According to Masego, in order to free Darla from her affliction, they would need to perform a ritual that would call upon the power of the Loa—the spirits of Vodun—to restore balance and drive away any lingering darkness. Alice trembled in fear at the thought of what Masego had proposed, until she saw Leo's determined expression. She knew this was their chance to save his mother and, with a deep breath of courage, Alice followed Masego's instructions, assembling everything required for the ritual—candles dripping wax, fragrant incense sticks and herbs filling the air with an eerie aroma, spiritual artifacts glowing in anticipation as they prepared to confront the unknown. Finally, they were ready to begin, but not without a chill of terror lingering in the air. Leo stepped forward first; his hands shaking slightly as he lit the candles one by one in a circle around him. Debbie followed next with incense which she lit and placed in different corners of the room while Alice carefully sprinkled herbs of Black Witch Powder Sage, Goofer Dust and Wild Harvest Herbs around the ritual space according to instructions given by Masego. Finally, when everything was ready, Masego read out loud the words of the spell. (Me-Kata-Dembela-Lay-Whinkitta-Dermosha-Wyatta-Keeyaka)

After finishing there was silence. The air in the hut grew stale, with nutting but the smell of burning herbs in the air. "It didn't work!!" Leo said as he dropped to his knees. "You aren't the one to do this child... She is!!" Masego pointed to Debbie as she stared into her soul. "Leo, you have the power of your mother running through your veins, but She is a direct descendant of Loa." She asked Debbie, "has she always felt surrounded by spirits and drawn to the dead?" Debbie answered, "Yes, since I was a child, I always felt safe in the cemetery. Debbie's fears had been confirmed; she was a descendant of the Loa, and it was her destiny to free Darla from her affliction. Tears streamed down Debbie's face as she faced the truth, but Masego comforted her with words of courage and strength. Despite her fears, Debbie nodded in acceptance and looked to Leo for reassurance. Masego then went on to explain that Debbie must first confront the darkness within herself before she could help Darla. To do this, Debbie must embark upon a spiritual journey to uncover the secrets of her past and to unlock the power of the Loa within her. She must confront whatever evil lurks deep in her dreamscape and only then can she hope to save Darla. The ritual began with an invocation to call forth the spirits of Vodun, after which Masego instructed Debbie to close her eyes and enter a meditative state. As soon as she did so, images filled her mind—strange people, dark places, flashes of Deja vu—but most of all fear overwhelmed Debbie as a voice whispered in her ear; "You are cursed." Horrified by what she had heard, Debbie opened her eyes and looked desperately at Masego for answers but there were none forthcoming other than "the truth is yours to discover." Unsure of how or why this had happened, all Debbie could think was that she needed to find out what these dreams meant in order to save Darla from whatever darkness lay ahead. The group stared in horror at

Masego, for they knew what she was suggesting. "I have to bring some thunder sage and Meranger roots with me to help" Masego said to the crew. She let them know this will provide more power to the spells they will need to cast. If they failed in their ritual, Darla would be cursed to an eternity of pain and suffering as a Knight of Hell, much too powerful and evil to be subdued. Leo, Debbie and Masego discussed their plan to enter the United States. Leo suggested they travel by cruise boat to avoid detection and offered up an old friend who had connections to get on the Carnival cruise line boat as workers, so that it could take them from Mexico into New Orleans. Once there, they would have to find a way to get off the boat without them and Masego being detected. Before they left, Leo handed Debbie a strange necklace with a powerful and mysterious sigil on it. He told her it was a protection talisman given to him by his mother for safekeeping when he was a child. He said she must wear it at all times as it would act as her guide and protector in her journey ahead. Masego urgently reminded the group of their time-sensitive mission and urged them to leave for Cozumel as soon as possible. She knew they needed to make up for the lost time to achieve success. The group rushed back to town and boarded a plane, destined for Louis Lopez's home in Cozumel. Leo had met him when Louis stayed with his grandparents who had immigrated to New Orleans. Although he was always getting into trouble in New Orleans, his grandparents decided the best thing would be for him to live back with his parents in Cozumel. With his many contacts and status on the island as 'jack of all trades,' it would not take long for Louis to get the crew uniforms and passage on a cruise boat out of the harbor. Soon enough, after suiting up, they made their way down to the docks where they boarded the large vessel which set sail towards New Orleans without delay. The boat finally docked in New Orleans and Alice, Leo, Debbie and Masego disembarked as quickly as possible. But Masego's lack of official documents meant that getting through US Customs was going to be a challenge. After creating a commotion at the loading dock, Debbie managed to sneak Masego past the Port Authority and security as Alice and Leo distracted them with their ruckus. Now officially in the US, Debbie felt a mixture of excitement and dread as they headed deeper into New Orleans towards Marcus's home. Soon they would set off on the long journey to their final destination, Darla's accursed home in Bayou Lafourche.

******

Chapter 7" Who Am I?

(A week earlier)

The crime scene glowed with the flashing lights of police vehicles, their sirens screaming into the night. In a sickeningly familiar sight, Marcus saw Dorian Miller's body slumped in his car along with his wife and two daughters, all gunned down mercilessly. Two shots to the head of the driver, while the others suffered head shot wounds and body shots — it could only be the handiwork of a professional killer. Marcus felt dread wash over him as he realized that this was the same type of hit, he had not seen since 2017. Everywhere he looked were members of SWAT, FBI, Local PD, Fire, EMS, and surrounding services attending to those injured in an attempt to flee from the sniper's deadly aim. Marcus has been tracking the nefarious activities of Apex 8, an organization led by Jabari - a shadowy figure shrouded in mystery. Apex 8 masquerades as a legitimate global producer of Nanotech and security, but in truth, it peddles weapons of mass destruction to terrorist nations wanting to gain control over the world's wealth and economies. With each step Marcus takes closer to uncovering their secrets, he knows all too well that his life hangs on thin thread. They are known for hiring trained mercenaries to do their dirty work for them. This was a similar hit and a nasty one. Marcus maneuvered around and gathered all the intel he could while letting the local departments handle their scene. Marcus scrambled to sift through the intel while informing local officials of their area's developments. All of a sudden, his phone blared out Sheriff Ratcliff's urgent plea from Bayou Lafourche

(Phone rings... Marcus answers)

Marcus: "Duncan here, What Can I Do for You?!"

Sheriff Ratcliff:" Agent Duncan, It's Sheriff Ratcliff. Things have taken an unexpected turn out here in Lafourche Parish. Three officers and a carjacker were savagely murdered almost beyond recognition. I think it was the same perpetrator you've been following. Also, one of my Detectives, Archie Davis, home and family was attacked by some large beast."

Marcus: "No way!! I'm in Baton Rouge but I'll race out there as fast as I can. Don't let anyone touch that crime scene! Take pictures, collect evidence - anything you find send me copies!"

Sheriff Ratcliff: You got it, Agent Duncan... See you soon.

(Both hang up phones)

Marcus arrived at the crime scene an hour later. The sight of four victims murdered in cold blood chilled him to the bone. Sheriff Ratcliff briefed him on the situation, and Marcus quickly sprang into action, gathering evidence and details of the crime. He looked over each body carefully and noticed similarities between this crime scene and the one when Agent Morrison and the other agents were attacked. "This has got the work of the Voodoo Lady in Black!!! Leo's mom is getting worse and deadlier." Marcus said to himself as he put on some gloves and sifted through the crime scene for familiar markers. Sheriff Ratcliff's voice was laced with a curious tone as he asked, "You really believe there is an evil monstrous lady that's killing folks with black magic in these marshes and bayous, Agent Duncan?" Marcus, who was more focused on finding proof, looked up. He responded to Sheriff Ratcliff, his voice low, resonating like thunder. "This is Louisiana, a place where shit just happens, and people are murdered by something scary!!" With those words hanging in the humid air, he went back to combing through the crime scene. Marcus and Sheriff Ratcliff were both on the lookout for clues that might lead them to the identity of the perpetrator. Marcus noticed a strange symbol carved into one of the victims, which he recognized as a voodoo hex sign. He also found a scrap of cloth from an article of clothing with strange esoteric symbols. Marcus knew then that they were dealing with a dark and powerful force. Marcus surged to his feet, eyes blazing, and fists clenched. "This has to be that same damn lady that attacked us and killed my agents plus that damn beast you seen is for her too," he raged. "The Voodoo Lady in Black right Agent Duncan," Sheriff Ratcliff mocked, but Marcus cut him off with a bitter laugh. "Don't insult my intelligence, Sheriff. This mutha fucker took out four of your men--was THAT real enough for you?" He spoke his truth as he yanked off his gloves, storming towards his car with a venomous rage, but Sheriff Ratcliff followed him, keeping his distance as he said, "What do you mean by 'mutha fucker'? Do you think it's a voodoo ritual of some sort? I mean the beast could have been a bear that attacked Davis and his family!!" Marcus stopped in his tracks and turned to face the Sheriff. He was seething with rage. "I don't know what it is, but I can tell you that it isn't good! We're dealing with some dark and powerful force here and we have to find out who or what is responsible before more people get killed." Sheriff Ratcliff nodded in silent agreement. Marcus continued, thinking aloud. "We need to track down this Voodoo Lady in Black and from our last dance, my partner Agent Morrison and two other friends has a plan to get rid of her ass once and for all.

Marcus glanced at his watch and cursed under his breath. It was already late, and he had a lot of work to do before morning, but he knew that every second they waste could mean someone else getting hurt or even killed by this mysterious woman. "I can't wait to hear from Debbie, Alice and Leo... I hope they come back with something powerful enough to kill this lady!" Marcus said to himself as he told Sheriff Ratcliff, "You better have a great amount of faith that those three can at least figure out how to kill her." The sheriff then apologized for the sarcastic comment earlier about if the Voodoo Lady were real or not, and Marcus said he would be attending the funerals of the fallen Officers on Saturday coming. The day arrived. Its Saturday morning, and Marcus and Sheriff Ratcliff drove to the funeral of the officers who had been killed by the mysterious Voodoo Lady in Black. The mood was somber and all those in attendance could feel the heavy weight of grief pressing down upon them. It was a time for sadness, but also a time for remembrance, and after saying one last goodbye and watching their coffins be lowered into the ground, they would go on with their lives. As they prepared to leave the ceremony, Marcus spotted a cloaked figure lurking in the shadows of a nearby tree. His heart leapt as he recognized Darla beneath her long black hood. "Who's that?" Sheriff Ratcliff asked as he pulled out his keys. "Now you believe me!" Marcus yelled before turning back to face her. She stood very still, her eyes glowing like red embers. Outlined on either side of Darla were two huge beasts, snarling and growling. With a sickening cackle she pointed at them both and vanished into the night. Sheriff Ratcliff frantically yelled out curses as he fumbled with his keys, desperately trying to snatch up his twelve gauge. He leapt into the car and shouted out to

Agent Duncan, "Please God, whatever plan you have with your friends, hurry it up! I am going to the local church to pray and implore for help. Agent Duncan, this stays between us until we get rid of this fiend. Count me in! But first, I need to talk to God right now!!" Marcus nodded in agreement and soon the Sheriff was out of sight, leaving him alone with his thoughts and plan. He knew that he had only one chance at saving not just himself but everyone else from this mysterious creature and so he quickly made his way back to his office where he could begin making calls. Marcus phoned Debbie, Alice, and Leo, who had just disembarked from the cruise ship with Masego. They were all pursuing their own inquiries and learning about Voodoo from the locals. Debbie told Marcus what happened while they were away, including Masego's help in curing Darla of her evilness. "I don't want her cured," Marcus said angrily, thinking of the agents killed and the four last week. After a heated debate over the phone, they eventually agreed on a plan to collect magical ingredients and create a spell powerful enough to annihilate her once and for all. Meanwhile, Sheriff Ratcliff arrived at the local church where he sought out spiritual guidance from Reverend James Smithson. The reverend listened intently as Ratcliff spoke about his encounter with Darla and all the destructions she had caused thus far. Reverend Smithson's eyes hardened as he listened to Sheriff Ratcliff, the desperation in his voice ringing loud and clear. He knew that divine intervention might not be enough this time - dark forces were at work here and something more potent was needed to combat it. Taking a deep breath, Sheriff Ratcliff told the Reverend about Marcus' idea to use a magical spell to rid the town of the dark entity. Reverend Smithson recalled his family had practiced Voodoo for generations and it was something he had always been scared of, hence why he had dedicated himself to serving the Lord. But he told Officer Ratcliff, "This was no different from an exorcism," and with a heavy heart, he agreed to help them gather together all the ingredients necessary for the powerful spell. Before sending him off, he warned them that it would take immense courage and fortitude to succeed.

******

It was late in the evening when Debbie called Marcus and said they were down the street from his home. Marcus prepared his home for their arrival, picking up all of the papers and case files, clothes and trash that was laying around. "Damn I can't believe I got my home this damn dirty. Marcus said as he laughed to himself. Suddenly there was a knock on the door. It was Debbie, Alice, and Leo, along with Masego, who was still dressed as a ship housekeeper. "Hey Marcus!!" Debbie said with excitement, showing that she missed him and was glad to be back in his arms. "Hey Leo, Alice and who's your friend here?" Marcus said as he extended his hands to greet Masego. "This is Masego from the village of Shangana. You would not believe what we did to get her into the country!!" Debbie said as she looked over at Leo and Alice and laughed. "What did you guys do?" Marcus asked. "We managed to sneak her in on a cruise ship, and then all of us sneaked back into port of New Orleans." After hearing the story of how Masego got to the city, Marcus was intrigued by her knowledge and asked for more information. To his surprise, she told him that she has vast spells along with knowledge of the

Handbook of Ritual Power and is there to help them entrap Darla's soul from the evil that binds her. Everyone started feeling a little at ease knowing they had at least a fighting chance. Masego was warmly welcomed as one of their own and Marcus asked her what she knew about Darla. She revealed that she felt the shift in the spirit world, as did all Sangomas. She felt the evil presence enter this realm and take possession of Darla. This is a powerful spirit, bound to a dark force by evil that only spells can remove from the Book of Ritual Power. The group was eager to learn more from Masego. After some questioning, it became clear that Masego had studied this book for years and she could offer them insight into how to break the binding spell and free Darla from its clutches. They all knew they must follow her instructions carefully as any misstep could be disastrous. She started by teaching them about the ritual components – the incantation, special symbols, and offerings that would need to be completed before they could reach their goal. She also advised them on what items they would need to purchase in order to complete the ritual, such as special herbs, candles, oils, and potions. Masego's tone then shifted as she began explaining the ritual components that were needed to break Darla's bindings. She was extremely knowledgeable about the subject matter and spoke with authority, which made everyone hang on to her every word. She quickly began to speak of the enchantment, brandishing symbols in a whirlwind and explaining various offerings that would be necessary for them to succeed. She detailed what items they must acquire in order to enact the ritual, from mysterious herbs to deceptively benign-looking candles and oils to unknown potions. Suddenly Masego stopped her frenzied recitation and went into a trance. The entire crew stood still, mesmerized by Masego's transformation as her eyes rolled back into her head. In a deep voice reverberating across the room, she intoned, "I must caution you once more: only the ancestor of Loa can perform this spell and that person is you, Debbie. You must find your family and learn the truth about your heritage. "Debbie was shocked by Masego's words and stared in disbelief. She knew that she must face the truth of her lineage, even though it was something she had been running from all her life. The others were in awe of the mysticism surrounding them and wondered if they could free Darla with such power.

Masego continued, "The ancestor of Loa is a powerful witch who can open the way to another world and call upon their ancestors to assist them in their spell work. You must reconnect with this power within you, or you will fail." Everyone felt a chill run through them as Masego explained what Debbie would have to do before they could move forward with the ritual. After a few moments, she snapped out of her trance and began to explain the details of the ritual one more time. She showed them how to draw specific symbols, create offerings, and recite incantations that would help break Darla's binding. Then Masego paused and looked directly at Debbie, telling her that once these steps were completed correctly, only then could she tap into her ancestor's power and complete the spell. Debbie nodded in agreement; she was prepared to make this journey alone if need be. She still had a lot of questions though: How can I find my ancestors? What will happen when I do? Will I be able to break Darla's bindings? Masego smiled knowingly at Debbie's confusion before continuing her instructions for the others. She explained that they must remain focused on aiding Debbie while she went through the process of finding her ancestors and unlocking her own powers. Everyone else promised to stay united and help Debbie if needed, while also trying not to make any mistakes on their end; they did not want anything standing between them and freeing Darla from her prison! Masego then offered one last piece of advice: "Be mindful of your words, for even when you are alone in the dark, your thoughts can still be heard." Marcus proposed they call it a night and reconvene in the morning. "The ladies can have my room, Leo and I will take the sofas, and Masego can use the guest bedroom," he offered. He then turned to Debbie and gave her a hug. "Tomorrow you should go see your mom and find out if there is any connection between your family history and Loa," Marcus suggested as Debbie began to get emotional. With Loa being a powerful Priestess, your mom should be able to give you some information on Loa being your family. Debbie was touched by Marcus's generous offer; it meant a lot that he cared about her enough to make sure she had a roof over her head. With newfound determination, she thanked everyone and wished them a good night before heading to the bedroom. In the morning, Debbie rose early and prepared for her journey to visit her mother. She knew this was an important first step in discovering more about Loa and her family history. She hesitated as she grabbed the door handle, then took a deep breath and stepped outside into the warm sunlight. Debbie could not help but feel excited as she drove towards her childhood home; it had been so long since she'd seen her mother. When she arrived, the memories came flooding back –the good times they had shared here when she was growing up. As Debbie stepped out of the car, her heart filled with warmth as she spotted her mother standing in the driveway waiting for her. The two embraced tightly before making their way inside. Her mother welcomed Debbie home with open arms and listened intently as Debbie asked about Loa and their family's connection to witchcraft. Her mother slowly shook her head before answering, "I'm sorry I don't know much about Loa or our ancestors' connection to witchcraft." Debbie sighed heavily in disappointment but still thanked her mother. She then Stopped Debbie and said, "I suddenly remember a small journal my mom, your grandmother, used to tell me about. It said that in every generation, there are two twin girls. Loa had a twin sister who was killed by a demon masquerading as an angel. In retaliation, she sold her soul to a crossroad demon in exchange for power to track down this angel. She found and killed it but became deranged and began murdering innocent people. The village folk captured her and burned her alive, and she cursed them with repeating generations of twins who will harness her power and avenge her for killing her. Debbie, my child, you had a twin who tragically passed away at birth. Debbie felt sick to her stomach as her mother recounted the story of her twin who had tragically passed away at birth. She had always wondered why she was drawn to witchcraft and now it made sense —she was the descendant of Loa, cursed with generations of twin births. Debbie asked her mother if there were any clues in the journal that could help her find out more about Loa. Her mom told her that she had read a few pages about a mysterious woman named Selene —Who she later found out was the crossroads demon, she was the one responsible for bringing Loa's power to life. She suggested that Debbie look into Selene's past in hopes of finding more answers. With newfound optimism, Debbie thanked her mom before leaving for home. On the drive home, Debbie thought hard about what she had learned from her mom and recalled reading a little bit about a crossroad demon named Selene in old journals about demons back in her college days. She recalled the passage written about a powerful priestess who could use their spells to summon powerful forces from beyond this world. Debbie remembered feeling drawn to this particular passage– maybe it was time to explore this side of herself further and take on the challenge of finding out more about Selene and Loa's family history! Debbie was determined to get some answers. She continued her research on Selene and scoured through ancient books, consulted with experts, and consulted the family journal for clues. After days of searching, she finally stumbled upon an old book that held the key she had been looking for –an ancient spell that could bind a demon and force it to answer her questions. Armed with this knowledge, Debbie set off at once in search of the crossroad demon. The journey was long and arduous but eventually Debbie found herself standing in front of a crossroads at midnight. Taking a deep breath, she read aloud from the ancient text and began casting a powerful spell. As soon as she finished the incantation, a figure appeared out of thin air –the crossroad demon Selene. Debbie shivered in fear at the sight of it but quickly gathered her courage and steeled her herself—she had come too far to turn back now. She demanded that the demon answer all her questions about Loa's family connection to witchcraft so that she could find out more about its power and use it to stop Darla. The demon agreed on one condition: Debbie must agree to become its host so that it could gain power from within her body while also helping her access Loa's power too. Agreeing to this bargain, Debbie confidently welcomed the spirit into her body and felt its power coursing through her veins–she was now connected with both Loa's spirit as well as with the crossroad demon's powers! Through their newfound bond, Debbie was finally able to uncover many secrets from Loa's world– including how to use magic safely and ethically to get rid of the evil that is in Darla. Debbie was ecstatic. Now that she had the demon's help, she could use magic to fight Darla and her ambitions of power and destruction. She thanked Selene for her cooperation before she disappeared in a puff of smoke. The force inside Debbie had become stronger than ever before, and she realized why she had been so pulled to the otherworldly. She was not completely certain if she was able to go against Darla, as the priestess was strong with doing Voodoo and Debbie was just a novice. So, she phoned Marcus and told him to make sure everyone was present so they could start. On her way back to Marcus's house, Debbie started seeing visions of Loa. She was a beautiful brown woman of Goddess stature, with ember red eyes and wore a beautiful African head and bead dress ensemble. Loa stood against a blinding light as she whispered to Debbie, "Eliminate everything that doesn't help you evolve, Own the power, don't let it own you!!" Then the bright light flashed as she swerved on the road and stopped on the side. Shaken by her powerful vision, Debbie pulled fully over and stepped out of the car to catch her breath. She looked up to the stars in the night sky and felt a sense of peace wash over her. She knew that she was meant to use Loa's power for good and protect the people around her from Darla's evil schemes. With newfound courage, she got back into her car and drove on to Marcus' house. Leo, Alice, Marcus and Masego were there and waiting to hear about what happened to Debbie. She explained what went on and asked Masego if she genuinely thought she was ready to take on Darla. Everyone seemed to hold their breath as they awaited her response. Without hesitation, Debbie confidently declared "Yes". Masego smiled at Debbie's resolute answer. She went into the guest bedroom and retrieved her potions, spell book, and other magical items needed for their plan of action. Marcus suggested that they contact Sheriff Ratcliff and Detective Davis of Bayou Lafourche to get insight on Darla's behavior. They agreed it would be wise to inform them of the situation and enlist their aid in blocking off roads that would lead to innocent people getting hurt during the confrontation. Meanwhile, Leo prepped their arsenal of weapons in case things got out of hand. Masego readied her voodoo spells that she believed could possibly weaken Darla's hold over her victims. Alice was preparing a large boiling pot filled with herbs and other materials for an energy shield to protect them from any physical or magical attacks that Darla might have planned for them. With all their preparation taken care of, everyone looked towards Debbie. Thinking back to Loa's words, she summoned all her courage and strength into her voice as she declared "Tonight we take down Darla!" Everyone nodded in agreement and set off to Bayou Lafourche. As they drove towards the bayou, the group discussed strategies on how they would take down Darla without anyone getting hurt or killed. When they arrived at the sheriff station, Sheriff Ratcliff was more than ready to assist them with manpower and support as well as forming a plan on taking out Darla and blocking off any routes that may be used by civilians getting caught up in their mission. "Good to see you again Agents, and your friends. I'm hoping all of this works to bring an end to the Voodoo

Lady in Blacks reign of terror here in Lafourche Parish." Sheriff Ratcliff spoke as he also let them know Detective Davis is out with a team covering interstate 10. They all showed their gratitude to the department, but they were all terrified about what was to come out there in them marshes. Once everybody was ready, they set off into the bayou under cover of nightfall where nobody could see them coming. The group moved stealthily around trees until they were close enough to barely make out what seemed like a ritual taking place within the dark fog surrounding them. Knowing now was their chance, Debbie gave a signal for everyone else to stay put while she walks forward alone... The fog grew thick and swirled around Debbie as she ventured closer to the old shack. Every step reeked of warning signs as she stepped over a pile of broken tree limbs and sunk into the murky marsh water. She pushed forward, all of her instincts screaming at her not to proceed. But before she could stop herself, she found herself in front of the same pile of branches again. Fear started to set in, and the realization hit her that she was stuck in some kind of loop - every time she stepped away from the pile, she was drawn back there as if by an unseen force. Debbie knew she was in trouble. As she neared the old shack, the loop seemed to be getting stronger and making it harder for her to move away from it. She closed her eyes and focused on channeling her strength into breaking out of the spell. Finally, after a few moments of intense concentration, she felt a slight release and opened her eyes. The fog had cleared, and she was standing directly in front of the shack. Debbie cautiously stepped forward until she reached the door. Taking a deep breath, she reached out and pushed open the door with trembling hands. Inside was darkness, but Debbie could make out a single figure standing in the center of what seemed to be an altar - Darla! Her face twisted in rage as Debbie entered, and she hurled raging words at her. "You fool! How dare you invade my sacred space!" Debbie stood tall despite her fear as she looked around. The walls were lined with various artifacts and trinkets, all seemingly devoted to some voodoo ritual or another. In the corner near Darla sat three wooden dolls with pins stuck in them -They were all representing Debbie's team members. Darla had obviously been using them as some kind of sacrifice or offering in order to maintain control over her victims in Bayou Lafourche Parish! The Crew drew near as they knew if they did not stay close, Debbie may become a victim of Darla's. And so... It was time for action - Debbie shouted for her team to join her inside as they rushed to the small opening outside of the front door of the shack. Masego wasted no time setting up a circle of protection around them while Leo quickly loaded their weapons with ammo that Sheriff Ratcliff had provided earlier that day. Alice set up an energy shield around everyone to prevent any physical or magical attacks from reaching them while they worked the counter spells right outside the front of the shack. Everything was strong within Darla's circle of spells. Taking a deep breath, Debbie stepped forward, her courage hardening to stone. "This ends now!" she declared. Darla's rage burst into an uncontrollable inferno, the heat in the shack intensifying until it was almost unbearable. A powerful gust of wind howled through the shanty shack, shaking the walls, and rattling its foundations with such force that even Debbie stumbled back in fear. Darla's eyes flashed with determination as she declared, "I won't let you defeat me... I will slaughter everyone you love before I let you take my life!!" A furious wind whipped around them both, like a maelstrom. Grunts and snarls echoed from the depths of Darla's loathsome Hell Hounds; her minions ready to battle. Debbie felt the fierce power of Loa surging inside her veins as she conjured her own diabolical pack of hounds, primed and ready to wage war against Darla's unholy beasts. The wind whipped around them as the two forces clashed, but neither had an edge and things seemed to be at a standstill. Debbie took a step forward, her voice booming in the small space of the shack. "This ends now!" Her words echoed off the walls as she summoned all her power and with one mighty wave of her hand, unleashed a powerful stream of fire that shot towards Darla. Darla's face contorted in rage as she countered with a wave of her own dark powers, sending a blast of icy frigid air towards Debbie. Despite the magical onslaught, Debbie held strong and continued to move forward. With each step she took, more and more fire consumed the area until it was almost too hot to bear. Debbie channeled her fear into a single attack of overwhelming power, summoning a raging storm that clashed with Darla's own assault. An eruption of blinding light thundered through the shack, shaking the forest, and momentarily blinding even the crew on the Interstate. When vision returned, Leo, Alice, Marcus, and the rest raced to the house to find there was no one there; Debbie and Darla had vanished in an instant. They both were gone….

The group stumbled back in shock and awe, looking around the empty shack in disbelief. Not a single sign of Darla or Debbie remained. In that moment, Leo realized what had happened. Debbie had used the last of her energy to break through the barrier between this world and the spirit world, taking them both away from danger and into a far-off realm of wonders beyond their comprehension.

Alice moved next to Marcus and placed a comforting hand on his shoulder as he wept for his lost friend. Leo put an arm around Alice, and they all stood there in silence, mourning what could have been. Finally, Leo spoke up, breaking the somber atmosphere with determination. "This isn't over yet," Leo said firmly. "We still have work to do here." Leo then turned to Masego and said "I will tap into my mother's power. I will learn the spells and all the rituals from you Masego if you will teach me. We have to find out what happened to them. No one just disappears like that... No one!!!" The only thing left to do was to collect the shards and accept the defeat. The small town had a long history, spanning back at least over two hundred years, and many of the people had grown up there. Naturally, they were shaken by what happened, but they were resilient. It took some time for the local officials and everyone else to restore order in the town. Leo asked the Sheriff not to demolish the decrepit shack, instead wishing to handle it himself. The Sheriff had agreed, reluctantly, as he did not care one way or the other because this was going to be a big unexplainable stain on Bayou Lafourche. The situation proved to be disastrous and almost inexplicable, as it was difficult to articulate to the public that a supernatural struggle had occurred in this isolated town.

****

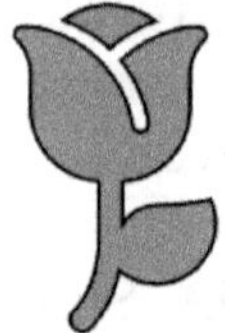

Chapter 8: Making Ways

It had been six weeks since the incident involving Debbie, and the remaining crewmates still felt the cold sting of her loss. Leo carried a deep inner hurt knowing that his mother had been responsible for so much destruction in Bayou Lafourche and was the notorious "Voodoo Lady in Black" responsible for many of the murders. When Leo heard Debbie's plea for help, he was filled with dread. He could see her as if looking through a window into another world, standing in the land of the dead where Darla held her captive. Gazing upon Debbie filled Leo with an all-consuming fear that spun his stomach and sent chills down his spine. He told Alice and Masego about it and gave Marcus a call to tell him about it all. Leo sat with Masego and asked to begin training with her. Masego had wanted to leave and go back, but she told Leo she would give his request some thought. Masego had stayed behind to teach Leo all she knew about Voodoo. The two of them immersed themselves in the dusty, old shack where the battle had taken place, poring over ancient books and scrolls. As he read more, Leo came to realize the strength and potential of this power. He began to comprehend that it was a powerful force that disregarded all conventions of race or religion. He witnessed the potency of the ritual, the proficiency of the priest or priestess, and their capacity to manipulate supernatural forces. Masego's vast presence provided comfort and solace to Leo throughout his training. She enlightened him with new knowledge he had never heard before, as well as showed him how to use these newfound powers safely. Every evening they talked until late into the night - Leo was captivated by Masego's mysterious incantations and chants. She also let Alice accompany her lessons, teaching her how to mix and create potions and herbal soups, as well as healing and protection spells. Alice studied all the myths and demons associated with Voodoo. And as the days and weeks passed, Leo gradually began to feel less and less alone in the world. He knew that with Masego by his side, he could take on the challenge. Marcus walked into the Bureau with his head held high, but he could feel the cold stares of his colleagues on him. He knew they were suspicious of him, thanks to his involvement in Debbie's disappearance. He was no stranger to scrutiny; having been an investigator for many years, he had faced it before. But never like this. It seemed like everyone had their eyes on him, judging him without giving him a chance to explain himself. He made his way to his office in silence, not stopping or looking around even once. He wanted to avoid any further confrontation with his co-workers and hoped that if he kept moving, they would eventually leave him alone. Once inside his office, Marcus began going through some paperwork on the case he had been working on prior to Debbie's disappearance—a series of robberies on the dockside that had gone unsolved for months. But this case seemed so insignificant now in light of the events that occurred in Bayou Lafourche. With a sigh, Marcus pushed away from his desk and stood up to stretch out the tension that had built up in his back and neck. He looked out at the cityscape beyond the window—all those lives and all those stories…and yet here he was stuck in one moment while all of life moved on around him. He remembered what Leo and Alice said before—that only together can they find Debbie and defeat Darla; but it felt impossible right now as long as he was being investigated for possible involvement with her disappearance. Marcus knew that if he wanted any chance of saving Debbie and putting an end to Darla's reign of terror then he needed help from some outside sources—namely Leo, Alice and Masego who already vowed to help with the investigation into Debbie's whereabouts. He also knew that if these three could be trusted then there was still hope for them all; hope that led them one step closer to putting an end to Darla. Despite their best efforts and all the time spent training, Marcus's search for Debbie continued to remain fruitless. Day after day he scoured the city, pouring through leads and tracking down potential clues with no tangible results to show for it. He was exhausted and beginning to feel hopeless, but something kept him going—the hope of finding Debbie alive and well. Leo and Alice both had jobs at the University of New Orleans during the week. Leo was a professor, teaching his classes on campus. He worked hard to make sure his students learned the best he could possibly teach them. Meanwhile, Alice worked as an assistant librarian at the University's library. Despite its hours, she thoroughly enjoyed her job where she could help students find books and research materials they needed for their studies. On the weekends, they would travel to Bayou Lafourche for training with Masego. They trained hard and honed their skills using every ounce of energy they could to become better. The visions of Debbie continued to haunt Leo, begging him to help her, save her from the realm of death. Leo was giving a lecture about ancient literature to his students when all of a sudden, he heard a strange noise: it sounded like chanting, but it seemed to be coming from the back of the classroom. As he turned around, Leo noticed one of his female students had risen from her seat and was now standing in the center of the room, surrounded by an ominous dark aura. She seemed to be in some kind of trance, her eyes glazed over with a distant look and her mouth moving almost as if it was writing its own words in a strange language. The chanting grew louder, and the student began to float up off the ground. Blood started coming out of her eyes and ears as she screamed out "Help me Leo...help me PLEASE!" Leo's heart raced as he tried to make sense of what was happening before him; could this be Debbie trying to reach out? He immediately ran towards her but before he could get close enough, she vanished into thin air leaving nothing behind except for an eerie chill that lingered in the room. Leo's heart was still racing as he was left standing in the middle of the class with all of the students looking at him. Small talk and giggles could be heard from the students. Leo then quickly cut the class short, not wanting to scare his students or embarrass himself any further. On the way back home, all he could think of was Debbie and the strange occurrences in the classroom. He knew he had to tell Alice and Masego what he had witnessed so they could figure out what it meant. When Leo arrived at his house, both Alice and Masego were already there waiting for him. After telling them about everything that happened in the classroom, Masego looked thoughtful for a few moments before saying "I believe this is a sign that Debbie is trying to reach out to you somehow, though I can't say what exactly she wants or how we can help her." Alice then suggested that maybe Debbie had been abducted by a much more powerful demon who was using dark magic which would explain why she seemed to be under some kind of trance. "We have to call Marcus and tell him. This is something he needs to hear.

(Earlier that same day)

Marcus was seated at his desk, reviewing the case of the Politian family from Baton Rouge who had been murdered by a hired assassin. At the time, only a handful of agents were in the office. Some of them were working on documents, one was on the telephone, and another was tidying up their workstation. For some reason, things fell off—the lack of conversation was almost palpable. Suddenly, everything went still, the lights flickered off and then back on again. Marcus found himself all alone: an eerie whisper filled the room. "Marcus help!! Help me, Marcus!!" she cried out. Marcus jumped up and grabbed his firearm, shouting, "Who's there? Stop playing around!" Marcus was in shock, the chill in the room had suddenly intensified. He could feel the presence of something dark and evil. "Who's there?!" he shouted again, trying to keep his composure as fear slowly crept up his spine. Suddenly a voice called out again from the darkness, "Marcus help! Help me, Marcus!" Marcus quickly pulled out his firearm completely and rushed towards where he thought the voice was coming from. He shined a light in the direction of the voice only to find it was Debbie, levitating a few feet off the ground with her eyes glazed over and her mouth mumbling strange words in an unknown language. As he got closer, she began to change into Darla. Suddenly, a deep guttural voice spoke from within the shadows and said, "I have her now and you cannot save her. She is mine!" Marcus looked around frantically for the source of the voice but could not see anyone. He then realized that whatever had taken Debbie was using dark magic to control her. The voice spoke again, "I have her now and you cannot save her. She is mine!" Marcus quickly turned his gun in all directions, but the shadowy figures laughed at him and faded away into the darkness. Again, the lights flickered on and off, then they stayed on. Marcus was left standing in the middle of the office sweating holding his gun. The blurry shape of other agents became clear, and they were seated at their desks all staring in his direction. "Marcus..." one paused while standing up from his seat in alarm. "Marcus... are you ok man?" "Ahh... yeah, yeah!" Marcus said as he waved them off and wiped the sweat off his forehead with his sleeve and headed back to his desk.

After a few hours had elapsed, Marcus was calming down from his experience. The captain suggested he look into counseling, assuming that Marcus was under pressure because of Debbie's disappearance. The shrill ring of the phone pierced the silence. Alice was on the other end, eager to share what happened to Leo at the university that day. She described how he had seen Debbie and then Darla had appeared out of nowhere. As Marcus listened, he told Alice about his own strange experiences. It seemed like Debbie was trying to reach out to them, but Darla was interfering somehow. The way the realm of reality slowed down for Marcus; it really had him shook. It was something he will never forget as he's, but it sparked a fire in him that won't go out until he saves Debbie.

******

Life was becoming increasingly strange, and Alice worried more and more about the events taking place around them. She had nightmares featuring Debbie and

Darla, but Leo did his best to keep her spirits up while secretly knowing something was off. He, Alice, Marcus and Masego needed to find a way to uncover the truth. All of them had been seeing Debbie and Darla in some shape form or fashion, but Masego was somehow protected from the harsh vivid visions the others had been experiencing. The fact that she had not seen Debbie and had any visions made her curious as to why just the three of them were targeted. The next day, Marcus, Alice, and Leo were discussing recent events. They had all been seeing Debbie and Darla in some shape or form, but Masego was somehow protected from the harsh vivid visions the others had been experiencing. The fact that she had not seen Debbie and having any visions made her curious as to why just the three of them were targeted. Alice suggested that if they could understand why this was happening, they might be able to find a way to save Debbie. She proposed that they go back to where it all began, Darla's house. "You think we will find any answers there?" Leo asked as he sipped on some herbal tea that Masego made. "I think we would!" Marcus answered. Masego bought the rest of them some of her herbal tea as they all sat around the table at Leo's house. Marcus, Alice, and Leo looked at each other in disbelief. They had gone this far to try to save Debbie and were willing to go the extra mile if needed. "We have no choice but to try," Marcus said resolutely. Masego nodded in agreement, adding, "We should prepare ourselves for the worst-case scenario. I have some powerful spells that could open a portal into the realm of the dead, but they come with great risk." She paused for a moment before continuing, "I'm sure there are other ways to enter this realm as well... Rituals or ancient magic." Alice's eyes lit up with excitement. "Are there any kind of spells or rituals we can use?" she asked eagerly. Masego nodded slowly. "Yes, but we have to really prepare, and we all might not make it back," she said gravely. All meaning the ones who choose to go inside the realm. That means somebody got to stay behind to make sure the portal stays open, and we get back out safely." Marcus stepped forward, volunteering himself for this task without hesitation. Despite his fear of what might happen inside the realm of death, he was determined to help Debbie escape from it and reunite with her friends. Alice and Leo agreed that Marcus' plan was the best one available and so they began preparing for their journey by gathering ingredients for Masego's spell and researching ancient rituals which could lead them into this dark place. After days of preparation, they were finally ready to set out on their quest - determined to find a way to bring Debbie back home safely. "So, we're really going to open up a portal into that house?" Leo asked Masego. "Yes, we are," she said as she stirred the herbs and powders together. "And hopefully it will work without bringing anything evil back with us." Marcus looked up at Masego and then panned over to Leo as he started packing more ingredients for the spells. "We don't need any more evil shit to happen to us!!" Marcus uttered. The crew sort of laughed at the way Marcus said that, not realizing that was the first time in days they actually laughed. "Tomorrow night we start, so we have to get into our "A" Game. We can't mess this up or we all die, well except for whoever stays behind." Leo said as he thought about coming into contact with his mother again. Masego sat still for a second, looking at them and said, "Alice will be the one to stay outside the portal because she knows the spells!" "Why me?" Alice asked Masego. "Because I've been training you all this time on how to mix and carry out rituals and potions.!" Masego said with a smile to Alice. Alice reluctantly agreed to stay behind while the rest of the group ventured into the realm of death. She was hesitant, but she knew it was the right thing to do. Masego reassured her that she would be safe and that she had been training her in preparations for this mission. Marcus gave Alice a hug before he left, assuring her that everything would work out in the end, and they would all be back together soon. "I'll see you guys' tomorrow night... I love you guys!!" Marcus said as he left to go home for the night. The group arrived at Darla's shack just after sunset and began to set up their spell casting circle.

"(Mayetta – Conwahyah- Dinday Lunguest- Perture- Kimesta LaTonga Ye)

Masego chanted ancient words while Leo lit candles around the perimeter and Marcus held a bowl of coal ready to create smoke signals should they need help. Finally, Masego finished her chant and suddenly a large portal appeared in front of them leading straight into the realm of death. Alice watched as her friends stepped through the portal one by one until it was only her left at the entrance of Darla's shack. She whispered a silent prayer for their safety before she closed off the entrance with a powerful sealing spell - hoping it would be enough to protect them from whatever dangers lurked inside. The portal was closing slowly so Alice could see what was going on for a few minutes. The group did not know what fate awaited them in this dark place, but they all hoped against hope that somehow Debbie could be saved from its grasp and that their own lives would not be taken away too soon. As the group stepped through the portal they were immediately met with a cold, dark atmosphere. They stumbled forward as they tried to get their bearings in the unfamiliar terrain. The air was heavy with a strange smell that seemed to be coming from everywhere, and a chill ran through their bodies that made them shiver despite the warmth of the night. The ground beneath their feet felt like stone, but the uneven and jagged rocks that littered it hinted at something sinister lurking somewhere in the shadows. Leo turned on a flashlight to help light their way and Marcus grabbed his Pistol, ready to defend them all if necessary. As they ventured forward, they heard strange noises coming from somewhere nearby - screams of terror mixed with laughter echoing off the walls, making them all uneasy about what lay ahead. Despite this ominous atmosphere, however, there was still hope that Debbie might be rescued - if they could find her before it was too late. As they trudged along, Masego started to chant an old spell - one that she said would guide them towards Debbie's location. After some time, walking through darkness and gloom, they finally found themselves face-to-face with a large stone archway leading into an unknown area beyond it. Leo cautiously stepped up to examine the ancient structure while Marcus stood back on guard. After some poking around he noticed a small piece of parchment stuck between two stones at its base - upon which was written: "Beyond this gateway lies an ancient temple of death; enter at your own peril". With one last look back at Alice standing vigilantly by the entrance of Darla's shack, Leo took a deep breath and stepped through accompanied by Masego and Marcus close behind him. The portal finally closed as Alice stared in with fear in her eyes. As they stepped through the archway, the group found themselves in a dark, dusty chamber. Leo shone his flashlight around, illuminating strange symbols and carvings on the walls. There was an eerie silence in the air that made each of them feel like they were being watched. Masego examined the symbols closely and determined that this must be some kind of temple dedicated to death, as indicated by the parchment they had found earlier. She also noticed that there seemed to be a large altar in the center of the room which could possibly hold Debbie or someone else important. The group cautiously moved forward, alert for any signs of danger. As they approached the altar, Leo noticed a figure lying on top of it - it was Debbie! She was unconscious and unresponsive to their calls, so Marcus rushed forward and gently lifted her off the altar while Masego kept watch. Heat engulfed the area as if the air itself was on fire, and Debbie's limp body was snatched from Marcus' arms and hurled onto the altar. The group immediately rushed forward to help her, but before they could do anything, Darla mysteriously materialized from the shadows. Her full African Priestess gown glistened in the twilight like the purest starlight, with sparkling beads and trinkets adorning it. Two vicious hell hounds circled them all hungrily, their menacing growls echoing off the walls. Darla laughed with a wicked glee that sent chills down everyone's spine and then she spoke: "Welcome to my temple of death! I am sure you've all had quite a journey to get here - too bad none of you will be leaving alive!" She cackled maniacally as she motioned for her hounds to move closer. Masego advanced and spoke a powerful incantation (Mateka-Domiya-Spratica-Dontama) that transferred a warrior spirit inside Leo while he tried to reason with his mother. Darla had fully embraced the dark side, and there was no hope of getting her back. Leo's breath caught in his throat as he felt the powerful energy of a warrior arise from within him. His face contorted into a fearsome mask of rage, and he was engulfed in a blinding white light. He emerged from the light dressed in an orange robe, bedecked with colorful beads that glowed with power. An aura of pure white light radiated from Leo as he grew larger, stronger, and more dangerous. He was ready to take on the evils of his mother and save Debbie and all who were threatened by her wickedness. Leo charged forward with a force that shook the temple walls, his newfound strength propelling him ever closer to Darla. The hell hounds snarled and leapt towards him, but he easily dispatched them with powerful blows from his fists. He roared in defiance as he faced off against the priestess, and a fierce battle ensued. Masego and Marcus used this distraction to carry Debbie away from the altar while Leo and Darla dueled. Darla was clearly outmatched by Leo's newfound abilities, and soon she was backed into a corner. She screamed in anger as Leo struck the final blow that sent her crashing onto the ground. With Darla seemingly defeated, Masego ran over to check on Debbie while Marcus tended to Leo who had collapsed in exhaustion after the fight. Thankfully, Masego was able to revive Debbie who awoke to find herself surrounded by her friends and family. The group prepared to leave the temple when suddenly they heard an ominous laughter coming from deep within its depths - it was Darla! She had risen again, more powerful than before and determined to keep her captives within her grasp. With an evil glint in her eye, she declared: "This is only the beginning of my revenge!" Having no other choice, the group ran back to the portal and escaped through it just as Darla raced towards them with a new swarm of hell hounds at her heels. Once they were all safely back in the shack, Alice acted and closed the portal before the void could flood out Not knowing that a hound got threw. They all took a moment to breathe a sigh of relief - they won this fight or so they thought. They finally made it back to the vehicle and just as fast as they got in the car, they drove off. The roads flew by as the car sped away from Lafourche parish. Marcus pressed down on the accelerator, determined to get everyone back home and back to their lives. He especially wanted to get the hell up out of the area. Alice and Leo were hugged tightly in the backseat, while Masego hummed softly to himself. Debbie found herself almost dozing off as she leaned against the driver's side window, until a large batch of trees in the swamp land caught her eye. Suddenly, Debbie saw something moving swiftly along the tree line, keeping pace with their car - a figure shrouded in darkness. Its steps were fast and furious, and it seemed intent on following them no matter how fast they drove. Debbie blinked hard and when she opened her eyes again, it was gone without a trace. She shook her head at her own imagination before settling back into slumber. But little did they know that somewhere in the distance, a hell hound growled menacingly amongst the shadows, hungry for its prey. The hound was hungry for its prey, but its mission was not solely to hunt and kill - it was also meant to keep them in its sights and scare them into submission. As Leo and his companions touched down in New Orleans, he could feel an unseen force lurking nearby. A chill ran through him as if a spectral creature were deliberately lurking within the shadows, its sinister gaze following their every move. The lingering atmosphere from the spirit realm seemed to hang heavy over the air like a cloak of fear, warning them that not all was as it seemed. Despite their efforts, it seemed like

Darla's pet had followed them back home and was not ready to let go of her revenge so easily. Marcus quickly led Alice and Leo back to his condominium while Debbie and Masego headed back to their home. All the while, the hell hound's presence seemed to be lurking around every corner. Debbie felt it. It felt like someone was watching them with malicious intent. (Hell, Hound sits and waits outside Debbie's home!! Growls)

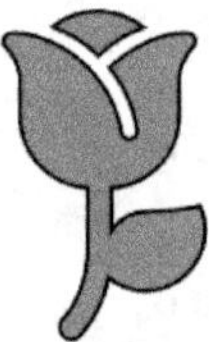

Conclusion:

(Back In the Realm of Death)

Darla was filled with a seething rage, her eyes blazed red and her teeth clenched tightly together. She had been defeated by Leo, her own son - a humiliation that burned inside her like molten lava. Her fists were clenched so tightly they shook, every fiber of her being infused with an uncontrollable fury. She wanted nothing more than to exact revenge on the one who had bested her; she wanted to cause them as much pain as they had caused her. In an act of desperation, Darla reached out to an old ally, a powerful demon known as Samael. If anyone could help her achieve retribution against Leo, it would be him. Samael agreed to help, offering Darla a way to send someone else in her place to do battle with Leo and his allies - a creature made up entirely of darkness - known only as the Shadow Beast. Darla knew this creature would prove invaluable in getting revenge on those who had wronged her, but she also knew it was dangerous and unpredictable; if not properly controlled it could turn on its master and wreak havoc across the land. Things not looking too good for Leo, Alice, Marcuse Debbie and Masego, because death is coming for them!!! The horror has only just begun. Darla will return with a rage beyond measure, her thirst for revenge unquenchable. Not even Leo, her beloved son, will be spared from her devastation and destruction. The ground trembles as she howls out a warning of damnation that echoes throughout the land –

no one will escape the consequences of their actions.

Death is coming and it will not be denied.

To be continued!!!!

A Bayou

The Story of Darla Gray

By

Eldon Raheem McCraine

www.ingramcontent.com/pod-product-compliance
Lightning Source LLC
Chambersburg PA
CBHW051522150726

47997CB00001B/348